Dueling Eagles

by Chad Clabo

© 2017 Chad Clabo
Minneapolis, MN
All Rights Reserved
http://www.clabo.net
ISBN: 978-0-9988043-5-4
Library of Congress Control Number: 2017904498

Cover design by Extended Imagery

Dueling Eagles

Chapter One

Ned Albrecht was used to waiting. He had spent more time waiting in his current position than in any employment he had ever held. Ned was three months in this new position, working as primary aide to Senator Michael Andreaz, and it didn't look like the waiting was likely to end anytime soon. Once this latest trouble on the border had started, the senator wasn't taking much time to deal with anything else.

The senator was currently in a meeting with five other senators and the President of the United States. Ned would prefer to be doing something, anything, other than waiting around for the meeting to end. The senator, however, wanted Ned to be immediately available, should something come up that might require his assistance. And being the senior senator from the Great State of Texas, he was going to require a lot of help given the current crisis.

The waiting room was pleasant enough. The chairs were comfortable, the decoration was agreeable, and Ned had gotten used to wearing a suit during the long campaign. Agreeable, thought Ned. That was exactly the word. This wasn't his first visit to the White House, but he'd never given it much thought before. The décor of the White House seemed, most importantly, not to offend. It was very agreeable. From the neutral colored walls, to the plush oversized chairs. Even the abstract patterns in the carpet weren't too abstract. Ned was about to get lost in one of those patterns when he heard the door to the oval office opening. Ned saw not only Senator Andreaz and his fellow senator from Texas exit the room, but also the two senators from California, as well as one senator each from both Arizona and New Mexico.

"Come on Ned," said the senator, as he walked quickly across the room. "We've got to get going."

"I thought you'd be in there for a while longer. What's going on?"

The senator remained silent, and appeared agitated. Ned thought it best to let the matter drop for the moment. They traveled down the halls and through security without any further conversation. It wasn't until they were alone in the back of the senator's town car that Ned decided to try again.

"What's happened Senator?" Ned knew that there was only one issue contentious enough to have caused this kind of reaction from the senator. "Is there a problem with the deportation program?"

"I don't know if it's a problem." The senator looked hesitant through the dim light of the darkened windows. "But it's definitely going to cause some waves. Ned, I want you to prepare for a flight back to Texas."

"I don't know if that's the best idea right now." Ned was trying to hide his surprise. "Sir, your calendar is full for the next two weeks, and there are several important votes coming up."

"No Ned, you misunderstand." The senator gave Ned a sideways glance. "We are not going to Texas. You are going to Texas."

"Texas?" said Ned in disbelief. "You've hardly let me out of your sight for the past three months, and now you're sending me to Texas?"

"I know you wanted to get a better feel for how things work in Washington Ned, but you've had four months here, and you'll be coming back."

"But what about Marlene? We have plans this weekend. She'd probably understand if I were accompanying you, but..."

"She'll still understand Ned. She knows the kind of work you do. I need someone at home who I can trust, someone who's going to give it to me straight, and without all the pandering."

Both men were silent for a moment.

"Okay," said Ned. "Texas. So what's going on anyway?"

"The president," the senator stopped, then started again. "The president has decided to accelerate the deportations."

"Accelerate? How does Mexico feel about that?" asked Ned, knowing that Mexico would not be happy. Mexico already wasn't happy. Even though the deportations were following a schedule that both governments had agreed to, Mexico's agreement was under threat of major trade embargoes.

"I'm pretty certain that Mexico doesn't know." The senator paused again. "And neither does anyone else Ned, so keep this quiet."

"But how long can we keep this quiet?" asked Ned. "People will notice an acceleration."

"Acceleration might be somewhat of an understatement," said the senator.

"Well then, exactly what kind of acceleration are we talking about?"

The senator looked contemplative, and after a moment, he answered. "The president is planning a mass deportation Ned, and it's happening tomorrow."

Chapter Two

"You have to leave today?" asked the voice on the other end of the telephone?

"I have to leave right now," said Ned. "I'm getting into a car as we speak, and it's taking me to the airport directly."

Contrary to what the senator had told Ned, it didn't sound like Marlene was very understanding.

"And you can't tell me where you're going, or why?" she asked.

"I already told you I'm going to Austin. As far as the reason, the senator wants me to keep this quiet for a few days. You know, national security and all."

"What kind of national security concerns can there be in Texas?" Almost as soon as she asked the question, she seemed to realize. "This has something to do with the border."

"Now don't read too much into what I say, Marlene. The bottom line is that I have to go to Texas, and I can't tell you why. Don't go trying to think that this is some kind of grand conspiracy."

Ned knew that Marlene was itching to turn this into a flashy news story. She was just getting started in the national news scene. Like Ned, she was new to Washington. That was probably one of the reasons that they seemed to get along so well. Both Washington outsiders, but both also wanting to be better connected. Marlene, however, had spent four years working in a Midwest newsroom cutting her teeth in the news industry, while Ned had spent most of that time campaigning in Texas for the senator's reelection.

"Grand conspiracy indeed," said Marlene. "You know, I'm not going out with you just so I can get a heads up on the political news of the day. I can wait for the press conference like everyone else."

"That's good to hear," said Ned. "I've been hoping that you wanted me for my body." Ned was only half joking. He had always kept himself fit, and his years in the military had kept him in good condition, but Ned knew that he was never going to win a modeling competition. He just wasn't that devoted to his appearance.

"Just keep hoping Ned, and be glad that your looks aren't your only positive attribute."

"More than one?" asked Ned. "That makes me want you to list them for me, but we just got to the airport. I've got to let you go. I'll call you as soon as I can tell you more about what's going on."

"Call me before then," said Marlene. "I don't know if you've heard, but my plans for this weekend just went out the window."

And with that, the conversation was over. Ned picked up his carryon bag and headed to security, the senator's office having printed his boarding passes before he left. In less than five hours, Ned Albrecht would be in Austin.

Chapter Three

Ned found himself waiting again. It had been sixteen hours since the senator's meeting with the president had ended, but it felt like it might have been only one. The flight to Austin went as smoothly as any other, and Ned was supposed to have had a brief meeting with the governor the previous night, but it was rescheduled for this morning.

How unlike this waiting room was from the one Ned had found himself in the day before. While it wasn't entirely disagreeable, there was a certain ostentatious swagger to Texas politicians, and it was reflected in their decoration. There was a painting commemorating what could only be the governor's alma mater, The University of Texas and their Longhorns football team. Opposite the painting, and directly behind the secretary's desk, was a pair of actual longhorns, mounted for display. Even mounted on the wall they looked like they could gore someone.

The secretary's phone rang; she picked it up, placed it back down, and told Ned that the governor was ready to see him.

"Ned Albrecht," Governor Arvin Foster shouted with his trademark enthusiasm. "I haven't seen you since last November. It looks like you forgot all your friends back home once your boss won his campaign." The governor grabbed Ned's hand and shook it with great gusto. "Sit down, Ned, sit down. I trust your flight went well. I'm sorry I had to cancel our meeting last night, but man, did I have a day."

"That's okay Governor," said Ned. "There's still plenty of time to get to El Paso?" Ned looked to the governor for confirmation.

"Oh yeah Ned, don't worry about that. I've got you on a military jumper at eleven o'clock. You should be there in time for a late lunch."

"And you've been fully briefed on the situation?" Ned once again looked to the governor.

"Yup, I was on a secure phone call with the president and his staff for almost an hour last night. I don't think I've ever spent that much time talking to el presidente before. Nothing like a crisis to get everybody communicating."

"Do you agree with the president that this is the best course of action? I know that Senator Andreaz has his reservations."

"Senator Mike," Governor Foster said. "Has reservations

about his morning coffee." The governor gave Ned a circumspect look. "But to answer your question, I don't know what the best thing to do right now is. There's no good solution to this problem. The food stores are going to be gone in less than two weeks, and that's only if we can keep filling them up at the current pace."

Ned knew that what the governor said was true. The Alien Relocation Center that had been built at Fort Bliss near El Paso was intended to hold only 10,000 individuals, but the number of people there now exceeded 20,000. There had been a stockpile of wheat and rice in October that would have fed 10,000 for more than six months. Now, it was six months later and the supply was nearly depleted, even after collecting additional food donations from across the country.

"Is there anything you want me to do while I'm out there?" Ned asked the governor.

"No Ned, I've got a man out there myself, he can handle anything I need." The governor stared out the window toward the skyline of downtown Austin. "I sort of wish I could go there myself, but those hounds in the media would say I'm abandoning my place of leadership during this time of crisis."

"True," said Ned. "But they'll say you're ignoring the problem if you don't go."

"That's right. You can't win for losing with those folks." The governor looked back toward Ned and then picked up his phone. "Jeanine, I want you to have my car ready downstairs to take Mr. Albrecht to the airport." He put the phone back down and then reached out to shake Ned's hand. "Listen Ned,

I want you to watch your back out there. El Paso's not the nice town it used to be. You keep yourself in the green zone, okay? We raised a lot of money together last year, and I'd hate to see you gone, just because you were stupid."

"Well then Governor," said Ned. "I'll try not to be stupid."

Chapter Four

While it wasn't Ned's first time on a military flight, it was the first time he had flown on one as a civilian. He couldn't get used to everyone calling him sir. He had thought about becoming an officer during his time in the military, and he almost certainly would have, had he stayed in, but the highest rank that Ned had attained while in the army was that of sergeant. Most of the passengers sharing this flight were soldiers headed to Fort Bliss for added security in support of the mass deportation, although it was likely that they didn't know exactly what was going on just yet. Except for Ned's conversations with the governor, no one seemed to know about anything out of the ordinary.

For the past six months, the Alien Relocation Center at El Paso had been sending four hundred LTAs across the border daily. LTA was the acronym used for those legally classified as Long Term Aliens. To be considered a Long Term Alien, the person had to have been residing in the United States for at least two years. The current expulsion agreement with Mexico allowed for not more than one thousand deportations of Long Term Aliens per day. Of that number, the El Paso Alien Relocation Center was allowed four hundred deportations daily. This number did not include STAs, or Short Term Aliens, of which there was no limit on the number that could be deported.

Once the plane had landed, Ned made his way across the dusty airfield and set out to see the base commander, one General Donato Everley. Ned had been assigned a local soldier as a guide and driver while on base, a Private Philips, and was very glad of it. He had visited El Paso once during the senator's reelection campaign, but they had never gotten to Fort Bliss, and it was also before the deportation center had been completely set up. Ned felt at once familiar with being on the military base, and also somewhat out of place. It seemed an incalculably long time since he had visited an army post, while in fact, it had only been four years since he had been released from active duty. Having finally arrived at the base headquarters, Private Philips introduced Ned to the general.

"General Everley," Ned said. "It's good to meet you. I only wish it could have been under better circumstances."

"Yeah, if wishes were horses, and all that." The general didn't seem up for the usual small talk. "Listen here Mr.

Albrecht. I've got less than six hours to get this operation underway, and orders to maintain secrecy. Do you know how difficult it is to give vague orders to people when you can't really tell them exactly what's going on?"

"Well…"

"I didn't think so," the general continued without waiting for Ned to finish. "So what can I do for you anyway? You have my full attention for exactly five minutes."

"Well," Ned started again. "What I really need from you is a brief understanding of how this operation is going to happen. I know that there is a plan for a mass deportation this evening, and that it is scheduled for approximately nineteen hundred hours, but I would like to know some of the logistics involved, as well as the final number of Long Term Aliens that will be deported."

"Operations won't be any different than a standard day, except for the numbers of course." The general sat down at his desk. It was a massive desk that divided the small room in half, but it looked decades old. Ned wasn't sure, but the room looked like it hadn't had a redesign since the time the building was built, although the paint looked fresh, with off-white walls to match the austere environment. "We're going to round them all up starting at seventeen hundred and then march them all down Old Highway Fifty-Four until we get to the drawbridge."

"But the Juárez officials won't be ready to take any more than the usual four hundred."

"No Mr. Albrecht," the general continued. "They won't

be ready, or willing I expect. That's why I've been authorized to send in an advance team to secure the Juárez side of the bridge. They will move in at eighteen hundred."

"You're conducting a military operation on Mexican soil?" asked Ned in disbelief. "Aren't you concerned that this is going to provoke a political response from Mexico City?"

"Everything about this operation is going to provoke a response from Mexico," The general said. "I don't make the policy here son, I just implement it. As for the actual number of deportees, I've been told that as a special representative of Senator Andreaz, you have clearance to receive this information, but I also need you to understand that this information is not cleared to be released in any format until this operation is complete. That is, no electronic or traditional correspondence of any kind. Don't mention it in a phone call, put it in an email, or even write it in your diary, is that understood?"

"Surely I can discuss this with the senator…"

"He should be cleared for this information in Washington, but it isn't something that should be discussed outside of secured communication, is that understood?"

"Yes sir," said Ned. "I understand."

"Good," said the general. "The number of deportees for today's mission is approximately fourteen thousand."

Chapter Five

Ned had been aghast. Fourteen thousand deportees. This number had provoked so many additional questions that Ned didn't know where to begin. Unfortunately, General Everley had insisted that their time was up, and even though he had set up a meeting with his civilian counterpart to address any further questions, Ned felt somewhat slighted by his brusqueness.

Once again, Ned was riding in the military transport vehicle with his driver. It was about ten miles from General Everley's office to the operational headquarters in El Paso. Most of the time was spent driving through Fort Bliss and around the El Paso International airport. Ned expected a war zone in El Paso, but the streets seemed quite settled.

"Is it always this quiet, Philips?" Ned asked the driver.

"I expect so sir, at least in the green zone," the driver replied. "But I don't get off the base too much these days, except for the deportations."

They were on their way to the former campus of the Texas Tech University Health Sciences Center, where the operational headquarters were located. Chosen for its proximity to the deportation port as well as the military base, the Health Sciences Center facility was a relatively new complex of buildings that supplied the civilian leadership of the operation a stable headquarters in the heart of the green zone. While the deportations were officially a joint operation with the military, the civilian command structure was supposed to be responsible for operational authority.

Driving through the city seemed like a rather normal affair, but Ned knew that the safe looking streets belied the reality of life in most of greater El Paso, as well as in Juárez, just across the border in Mexico. There were other cars on the street as they traveled down Airport Road, and the closer they got to downtown, the more people they could see walking. Ned knew that outside of the green zone, things would not be so normal. He had heard stories about gangs roaming the streets with little interference from the police, and knew that since the closing of all ports of entry between Juárez and El Paso, the crashing local economy had made the city's commercial viability all but nonexistent.

When they finally arrived at the operational headquarters, Ned found himself surprisingly impressed with the buildings. The capitol building in Austin was terribly grand, while the military buildings on the army post were extremely utilitarian. The buildings here seemed to blend the two styles somewhat gracefully. The brick exterior of the main building and the abundance of windows made for extremely well lit offices and conference rooms. Classrooms, Ned had to remind himself as he walked down the halls to meet with the director, they used to be classrooms.

Abigail Rodriguez was the civilian director of the Alien Relocation Center here in El Paso. When Ned arrived at her office, he was told that she was already speaking to a Mister Stuart, but that he should go on in. Her office had a very academic feel to it, which was almost certainly a holdover from when this had been the office of the president of the Health Sciences Center.

"Mister Albrecht," the director greeted Ned. Ned was a little surprised that she wasn't very tall. In his experience, most women in powerful positions were tall and at least a little imposing. Abigail Rodriguez was neither. "I'm glad that you've made it. I cleared some time in my schedule for both you and Mister Stuart, who arrived this morning. Have you met Mister Stuart?"

"I told you to call me Jack," said the other man in the room. "And I met Ned a couple of times last October, though we never really did get a chance to get acquainted.

Ned recognized Jack Stuart as one of the workers on the governor's reelection campaign, although, like he said, they didn't really know each other. Jack wore a dark suit that didn't quite fit, and his hair was a bit shaggy. This must be the governor's man in El Paso.

"And you both can call me Abby," said the director. "Why don't we all sit down? So Ned, I understand that you had a brief meeting with the general, but you probably still have questions."

"I'd say that was a bit of an understatement," said Ned. "That meeting left me with more questions than I had going in, and at the top of the list is, where did this fourteen thousand number come from?"

"Fourteen thousand?" asked Jack. "Is that how many y'all are sending back today?" Ned felt a little bit of relief that he wasn't the only one who was dismayed by this large number.

"Yes, fourteen thousand is the approximate number," said the director. "And yes, I realize that this seems like an insanely high figure. I argued against it. I told both the general and the president that the Juárez officials won't be able to handle anything like that number, but they insist on following this new formula, and..."

"Wait," said Ned, cutting the director off. "What's this about a new formula?"

"Well, you both know that according to last year's treaty there is no limit to the number of Short Term Aliens that we can deport, and that Mexico is responsible for transporting any Non Mexican Aliens through their territory if deemed suitable?" Director Rodriguez looked to both men as they nodded in agreement. "Up until now, we've been taking people at their word for how long they've been residing in this country, as well as their country of origin. The justification, therefore, for deporting so many, is that we are now classifying all those without proof of United States residency for more than two years as Short Term Aliens, and those without proof of Mexican citizenship as Non Mexican Aliens."

"Thereby appearing to hold to the letter of the treaty," said Ned. "While completely ignoring the spirit of it." Ned knew that the director had been correct. This sounded completely insane. "There is no way that Mexico is going to tolerate this. Has anyone given any thought to what their response is going to be?"

"I think the president's feeling is," said the director. "That they won't like it, but won't be able to do anything about it. With their trade being so heavily reliant on us, there isn't much that they can do."

"Yeah." Jack added his voice back into the conversation. "It isn't like we can·expect a military response from the Mexicans."

"This doesn't just sound insane," said Ned. "We're talking about the inability of the Mexican Government to form a military response? This is completely nuts. The United Nations would probably sanction us for this deportation if we didn't have our veto."

"You're probably right there Ned," said Jack. "It's a good thing we have that veto. Wait, did you hear that?" One quiet boom was followed quickly by several louder ones. Then the building shook.

"What the hell was that?"

Chapter Six

It wasn't very long after the first explosion that both the lights and the telephones went down, and not only the cellular devices, but the landlines as well. If it wasn't for the daylight streaming in through the cavernous windows the three had gathered around, they would almost certainly be working in the dark.

"What on earth could have caused this?" asked Director Rodriguez.

"Hell if I know," replied Jack. "Pardon my French, Miss Abby. You have any ideas Ned?"

"Well," said Ned. "If the entire electrical grid went down, that might cut the power to the cellular towers, but there should be some kind of backup, and the phone lines should still work despite an electrical grid failure. That's one reason that government offices continue to use landlines."

"And what about the explosions?" asked Jack.

"I don't know. IEDs? Domestic terrorism seems pretty unlikely, but," Ned paused barely a second. "Yeah, I don't know."

"What are we going to do?" Director Rodriguez was beginning to look panicked. "We're cut off from the military. If we can't talk to General Everley…"

"Wait," interrupted Ned. "You've got to have some kind of alternate way to contact the General. He wouldn't have left you here without some kind of military support, would he?"

The director moved to take her seat. "He wanted to assign an entire platoon here for security, but I wouldn't hear it. I made them set up…" Then her eyes became wide. "At the old health services clinic."

"And where exactly is this clinic?" asked Ned.

***

The old clinic was just a few blocks away from the administrative building. Ned, Jack, and the director soon found themselves in an emergency stairwell walking down three stories with only the built in flashlight from Ned's phone.

"At least the flashlight function on your phone still works," said Jack. "A silver lining in every dark cloud."

"For as long as the batteries hold out anyway," replied Ned. "Hate to rain on your silver lining Jack, but I'm not feeling so optimistic right at the moment."

They emerged from the stairwell into the ground floor

lobby. With even internal communications out, no one should have been expecting them, but a crowd had gathered in the lobby, and when they saw the director, they swarmed.

"Listen up everybody," said the director. "I want you all to remain calm. I'm going to visit the clinic in order to coordinate with the military staff there and reestablish communication with Fort Bliss. We'll figure out what's going on and I'll return with more information."

"Private Philips," Ned yelled to his driver. You're with us.

As they exited the building, they could see several clouds of smoke rising off in the distance.

"Philips," said Ned. "Do you know where this old clinic is?"

"Yes sir, I've been there before. And if I'm not mistaken, it's right over there." Philips pointed as they all turned to see a cloud of smoke rising only a short distance away.

"All right," said the director. "Let's not waste any more time."

All four of them climbed into the military vehicle and they proceeded to the clinic, but as soon as they arrived, they knew it was too late. There was only a burning pile of rubble where the clinic had once stood.

Chapter Seven

"Well, what do we do now?" Jack looked thoroughly frustrated.

"Philips," said Ned. "See if you can get the vehicle's communications system working. I'm going to scout the area for survivors."

"I'll come with you," said Jack. "You'll be okay here Abby?" He asked the director.

"Yes, you two go on. I'll stay here with Private Philips."

Ned looked back at the director. While none of them were dressed for reconnaissance, her suit skirt and heeled shoes made her outfit especially unsuitable.

"We won't be long," said Ned, as he and Jack began to walk the perimeter of the building.

The building looked as if it had been built mostly with

steel and concrete, but there must have been other materials used within, as pockets of flame appeared among the piles of broken concrete and mangled steel. The destruction wasn't confined to the foundation of the building either, as the debris spread out into the street and surrounding buildings. Ned didn't think that anything could have survived this kind of destruction.

"Over here," Jack shouted. Ned ran to join him. There were two bodies on the grass. The first looked burned beyond recognition. The other lie face down, looking mostly unharmed. "Here, help me turn her over." As they rolled the body, they could see she was injured much more severely on the other side. Her face was covered in cuts and bruises, and her uniform was bloodied and torn. Then she began to stir.

"Do you know where you are?" asked Ned. "Do you know what happened?"

"No," the soldier replied. "We were just coming back and…" She opened her eyes wide and started looking around. "What happened?"

"She's not going to be of much help," said Jack.

"No," said Ned. "Let's get her back to the vehicle. Maybe we can get her to a hospital."

"But what if she has, you know, internal injuries?"

"They're not going to get any better if we leave her here either." Ned waited for a reply that didn't come. "I can carry her by myself, but I'd appreciate your help."

"Okay, okay. But remember, this was your idea."

Private Philips was still working with the vehicle's

communication system when they returned.

"You found someone," the director said as they approached, carrying the soldier between them.

"She needs medical care." Ned replied. "You have any ideas?"

"I have a medic on staff back at the admin building, or there's a hospital just a block over."

"It's your call Director."

The director took a closer look at the soldier. "I think we'd better get her to the hospital."

"That sounds good," said Ned. "Philips?"

"Yes sir," replied Philips. "I know the way." Then he put the vehicle into reverse and headed back the way that they had entered.

"Did you get that comm system working, Philips?" asked Ned.

"No sir, the only thing that seems to be working is the GPS."

"You'd think they'd put some kind of emergency radio into these things," said Jack, once again looking thoroughly disgusted.

"Umm, sirs, ma'am," Private Philips looked over to his passengers.

"Yes private," the director replied.

"I just remembered. I think there might be a radio in the back."

"In the back?"

"Yes ma'am. In the storage compartment, in the back."

Chapter Eight

It didn't take long for the group to drop the wounded soldier at the hospital. After that, they returned to the director's office with the emergency radio.

The radio was in a green steel box about the size of a briefcase. The Army was still giving basic training in the use of standard communication radios, so it didn't take Private Philips too long to get it working. Because it ran on a standard twelve-volt system, the director sent a volunteer to commandeer a couple of car batteries so that they could keep it powered for an extended period if necessary.

"Have you gotten a hold of the general yet?" Director Rodriguez asked the private. Philips had been working his way up the chain of command.

"I think so ma'am," the private replied. "I've given his

lieutenant the rough details. We're waiting for him now. I think your name is the only one that would have gotten him on the radio. It sounds like they're almost as in the dark as we are."

"Well, that's not a good sign." Jack was slouching on a brown leather couch that ran along the far wall of the director's office.

"One other thing," the private added. "The lieutenant says that we are only to use first names or codenames during radio communication when possible, because while these frequencies are reserved for military use, they're simple analog transmissions that might be listened in on."

"I'd say he was paranoid under different circumstances," said the director. She looked over to Ned and Jack. Jack shrugged his shoulders.

"All right," she said. "I understand." They waited a few more minutes before the radio buzzed back to life.

"Sean, is that you?" The voice crackled on the other end of the radio call.

"Yes…" Private Philips answered into the radio. Ned was sure the private almost finished by adding "sir," but he resisted. "Yes, this is Sean. I'm here with Ned, Jack and Abby."

"Who knew the private had a first name?" Jack said quietly to Ned.

"All right, I'm going to keep this short and sweet." Again, the voice from the radio spoke. "Abby, I want you to prepare your people for evacuation. I'm going to send trucks out there to get you. We can't be sure that that location is safe."

"I don't think so." The director sounded adamant. "I'm not going to abandon my offices without some idea of what is going on? Just what is going on, Don?"

Don? Ned thought. Is that a codename? Donato Everley, Ned remembered the general's full name. Ned didn't think he'd ever be on a first name basis with a general, but here he was.

"While we're not exactly certain what's going on," the general continued. "We do know that the explosions were caused by missiles fired from the hills outside of Juárez, from the Mexican side of the Border."

"Missiles?" The director sounded shocked. "Don, what is going on?"

"Like I already said, we're not exactly certain. Our intelligence about what's going on in Juárez is obviously lacking. With communications out, we haven't been able to reach any of our assets there, and I'm not getting anything from any other sources." The general was being deliberately vague with them, but Ned knew that he probably meant the CIA wasn't giving him any information. "What we need is someone on the ground who could tell us what's going on, but I don't have anyone to spare."

Ned had a million questions that he knew he shouldn't ask on an open communications line. He condensed it down to one. "Don, this is Ned, is that something that I could do?"

"What?" asked the general. "Go to Mexico? Why would you want to do that?"

"I am supposed to be…" Ned paused to think. "My Boss's

eyes and ears here. I can't very well report to him if I don't know anything myself. Also, you said you needed someone on the ground."

"I don't know, Ned. This is highly irregular. Under normal circumstances I wouldn't dream of it, but maybe this isn't such a bad idea. I pulled your record before our meeting. You might be qualified for this kind of work, but you'll need someone along for backup. Maybe Sean could go with you."

"With all due respect," said Private Philips. "Maybe you should find someone who knows Juárez better than I do, someone who could act as a guide."

"That's probably a good idea. I'll see what I can do."

"Wait a minute." Jack had remained silent up until this point. "Maybe I could go. I don't have any special qualifications, but I do know Juárez like the back of my hand."

"Who is that?" asked the general.

"That's Jack," replied the director. "You know, from Austin."

"All right, that might work." The general paused. "Okay Abby, your people can stay there for now. I'm still sending a couple of trucks with supplies for you. I'm also going to send someone to brief and equip Ned and Jack before they leave. They should be there in less than an hour. Don't call me again until then. Over and out."

"That was abrupt," said the director.

"It certainly was," replied Ned. "Jack, what do you think? Is he holding something back from us?"

"Well Ned, I'm sure there's a whole lot he's not telling us, but we'll find out soon enough. There is one thing that I do know though." Jack looked at Ned with a sly smile. "It looks like you and I are going to Mexico."

Chapter Nine

The military trucks were carrying more than supplies for the administration building. There must have been fifty soldiers as well. They set up a perimeter around the building and even installed some kind of anti-missile device. Perhaps the most important things that the general sent were two satellite phones; one for the director, and one for Ned and Jack to take to Juárez.

As promised by the general, there was someone sent to brief and outfit Ned and Jack for their reconnaissance work in Mexico, one Captain Smith. He told them the plan for their insertion into Juárez, how to contact the general once they were there, and how to get back into El Paso, if they couldn't be extracted. More or less, they were expected to find out who launched the missiles and why, and to establish communication with one of the general's contacts in Juárez.

There was a pile of old clothes for them to choose from so that they would blend in better with the population of Juárez. Suits and ties didn't seem to be the uniform of the day in Old Mexico. Ned found a pair of blue jeans and a beat up jacket with a broken zipper. It would be plenty warm in daylight, but the jacket might come in handy if they couldn't find shelter for the night.

"You're going to want one of these," said Jack, as he handed Ned a cowboy hat that used to be white, but was now closer to a muddy yellow color." Fortunate or not, the hat was a bit too snug for Ned.

"Doesn't fit. What about this one?" Ned asked, holding up a weathered leather hat that was round and had a dark green hue to it.

"It'll do. You know, most Texans have a much better hat sense than you do." Jack was looking Ned up and down like he was suddenly out of place.

"Your instincts are correct," Ned replied. "My family was originally from Pennsylvania. My dad was stationed in Texas when I was in high school, but before that, I had never set foot in Texas."

"Well I might have known. Still, if you played high school football in Texas, I might be able to overlook your questionable origins."

"Third-string quarterback good enough for you Jack?"

"I suppose it'll have to be." He didn't look entirely convinced. Jack had removed his tie, changed his shoes, and dirtied his shirt, but otherwise hadn't changed clothing. Still, Jack looked completely different than he had a few hours ago. His shaggy hair was now completely disheveled, and it looked like he had suddenly become unshaven. The somewhat polished look of Jack's ill-fitting suit was completely gone as it now looked far too big, terribly worn, and completely out of place, along with his shabby shoes and dirty shirt.

"If you both are ready," Private Philips had just entered the room. "Then it's time to go."

***

They drove the several blocks up Alameda Avenue to what was the last official checkpoint on the deportation route. Philips had been joined by Captain Smith who was now driving the vehicle. Once they arrived, Ned marveled at the sight before them. Looking down at what used to be a four lane restricted access highway, it now looked like a river of people. There were manned guard towers every hundred meters and tall concrete barriers on either side of the road, leaving nowhere for the sea of people to go except forward.

"That's where we're inserting you." Captain Smith pointed to a guard tower by the highway. "You'll have to drop down from the barrier and blend in with the crowd." The captain had previously informed them that Mexico had cameras covering the entire border with the United States, and that anywhere they chose to cross would certainly be monitored. Blending in with the deportees was really the only surefire way to enter Juárez without being noticed. Even this plan relied on the assumption that the Mexican authorities would be too overwhelmed by the mass influx of deportees to notice a couple of people out of place. The general had supplied them with official deportation papers but, despite being authentic, they were based on phony information. Under scrutiny, they would not hold up.

"Wait a moment," Captain Smith touched his earpiece. "Uh-huh. Yeah. Uh-Huh. Damn."

"Okay guys, we have a bit of a situation here."

"Now what's goin' on?" Jack seemed to be losing most of his charm as the day went on.

"The advance team just secured the Juárez side of the bridge."

"Was there trouble?" asked Ned.

"No sir, no trouble. Zero trouble actually. That's what's strange. The Juárez side of the bridge was completely abandoned."

"So how does that change our plan?"

"It doesn't," said the captain. "The general says we should go ahead with the insertion. In fact, this will make it a lot easier. Without Mexican officials, we're just going to push the deportees out onto the streets of Juárez, and that means there won't be anyone to monitor you two going in."

"But wait," said Ned. "Without the Mexican officials, where are all these people going to go?"

"I know that fourteen thousand sounds like a lot of people, but greater Juárez has a population of over two million. Fourteen thousand more won't significantly increase the population. These people will probably spend the night on the streets, but they'll find somewhere to stay eventually, and long-term, it'll be better than staying at the relocation center."

"But Captain…" Ned started again.

"No sir," the captain interrupted. "I have to insist. This is the general's decision, and we have our orders. We're going ahead. Now are the two of you ready to go?"

Chapter Ten

Ned and Jack climbed the stairs to the guard tower and quickly dropped to the ground. With the sun still bright in the western sky, there was no way to be completely covert, but no one seemed to pay too much attention to the two men dropping in from over the edge of the barrier. Jack made some comment about the stupid soldiers dropping them over the wall without even bothering to check their paperwork in perfect Mexicano Spanish, and although neither Jack nor Ned looked at all Mexican, suddenly, Jack looked like this was exactly where he was supposed to be.

"What are you, some kind of chameleon?" Ned asked Jack in a hushed voice.

"Come on," said Jack, not answering. "Let's get ahead of anybody who might have seen us drop in. There'll only be more questions."

They pushed their way through the crowd as quickly as they could without raising suspicion. There was less than a mile to the drawbridge.

The drawbridge was the new border crossing built at the same time as the deportation camps. Nearly all other border crossings with Mexico in El Paso had been closed, and the drawbridge had been built as an exclusive deportation path into Mexico's new deportee acceptance center on the old campus of the Autonomous University of Ciudad Juárez. It wasn't in actuality a drawbridge. There were actually two massive wooden gates that opened or closed the bridge. Ned could see the gates pressed flat against the side of the highway as they approached the crossing.

Once they arrived, it was just as Captain Smith had said. There were no Mexican officials to be seen. There were, it seemed, a company of United States soldiers on either side of the highway beyond the Mexican side of the border, but they were maintaining their stations, just outside of United States territory.

As Ned and Jack proceeded into Juárez, the streets looked almost abandoned except for the new arrivals. Ned knew that the Juárez neighborhoods near the border had become as bad as those in El Paso. Again, the local economy was nearly non-existent and crime was rampant.

"Where do you think we should start?" asked Ned.

"Well," Jack replied. "The Pronaf District is just ahead of us here. When Juárez is doing well, it tends to attract the city's more progressive thinkers."

"You mean the party crowd." Ned knew that part of town that almost every city had.

"That's right, and while right now, that part of the city is filled with criminals, I think we're looking for a more organized kind of troublemaker. I suggest we head downtown; Centro, the locals call it. It's west of here. It's the commercial center of the city, and the place we're most likely to find some kind of community shelter without walking forever."

Ned could see the crowd starting to break up.

"We should tell these people to stick to larger groups," said Ned. "They're less likely to be preyed upon if they stick together."

"I hear you Ned, but if we're supposed to be blending in, we don't really want to set ourselves up as some kind of leaders down here, now do we?"

Ned knew that Jack was right, but he really wished there was something he could do to help these people.

"But maybe we can use that idea of a big group to help us get to where we need to go." Jack motioned to some of the crowd. "You see those folks? I bet they're just waiting for someone to tell them where to go."

Jack didn't wait for Ned's approval. "You all there, maybe we should stick together. Safety in numbers and all that. Why don't we head downtown. It's this way."

Chapter Eleven

Jack led the group downtown, stopping to ask any locals if they knew where he could find shelter. The group they were leading consisted of two families with children and one married couple. Jack had not only regained his charm, but had once again become a chameleon in Ned's eyes, speaking perfect Mexicano Spanish to the Juárez locals, and switching back to English for the group of deportees. Many of the deportee children were more fluent in English than Spanish and Jack probably would have gotten their entire life stories out of them if it hadn't been such a brief walk downtown.

As they approached the City Centro, there was more foot and automobile traffic on the streets. Jack kept asking the locals about shelter, and while some of them pointed the group to local churches, or to city hall, many were suggesting a warehouse shelter just west of downtown. Jack kept following the directions he was given and, before long, they arrived.

It was more of a complex of warehouses than just a single one. It seemed odd to Ned that the warehouses were seemingly new construction in this old part of the city. The long shadows of the evening sun had thrown the eastern side of the building into shade. There was a large sign there on the corrugated steel siding that said, "Esperamos Centro de Socorro."

The We Hope Relief Center, thought Ned. Not a very elegant name in either language.

As they entered the building, Ned could see that beyond a small reception area, there were hundreds of cots, and wondered if this was their everyday set-up. While it's true that it had been standard procedure for the past several months to send four hundred deportees into Juárez daily, Ned was under the impression that many of those were being bussed by the Mexican Government into other parts of the country. Still, he supposed, a room like this could fill up pretty quickly after several weeks of people coming in. In fact, he was somewhat surprised that the room wasn't already crowded with the city's homeless. Except for a few people milling around the periphery, the warehouse appeared almost empty. Ned was now happy that they had moved so quickly across the city. With fourteen thousand more behind them, he was glad that they had found shelter for at least this small group of deportees.

Several members of Ned's group began to unfurl the

papers they had been issued prior to leaving the United States to show to the man who was sitting at the desk. Jack was already speaking to the man in a quiet voice that Ned couldn't quite understand.

"Good news everybody," Jack said as he turned around. "They've got room for all of us. You don't need to show the man any papers, just sign the sheet, and find the bed that matches the number on the sheet."

Jack had already signed for both himself and for Ned.

"So we're spending the night here, I take it?" asked Ned.

"Unless you've a better idea," Jack replied. "I figure now we have this group settled, we should head back downtown and start making inquiries while the rest of this lot is finding supper. Maybe we can find supper too while we're at it. Isn't that how this spy stuff works?"

It was beginning to annoy Ned how Jack was taking the lead at almost every step. Still, he wasn't doing anything that Ned didn't agree with.

"Alright Jack, you take the lead."

There were now dozens more people heading into the building. As Ned and Jack were leaving, four men who were all dressed alike approached them. Ned could suddenly feel the barrel of a gun pressed into his back.

"We heard the American Army was sending spies," one of the men said. "So nice of you to come to our doorstep."

Chapter Twelve

Ned and Jack were brought to another warehouse together, but then quickly separated. Unlike the first building, this warehouse was divided off into many smaller rooms. The room they were holding Ned in was not a typical jail cell, but there was a steel barred wall with a gate in it running across the center of the long room. The rest of the room was made up of a concrete floor and unfinished drywall.

If only I had a screwdriver, thought Ned; or a heavy piece of metal, or a rock. He even contemplated punching through, but there was no telling what was inside the wall, or on the other side. Never mind the fact that there was an armed guard standing on the other side of the room. From the surface, however, the walls looked like standard wooden stud construction.

A man entered the room. He was dressed like the men who had brought them in, wearing blue cargo pants and a matching blue shirt. Now that Ned had a better chance to look at them, they looked somewhat reminiscent of military fatigues.

"I am here to inform you that you are now a prisoner of the Chihuahuan Liberation Army. As a representative of the United States Government, you will be put on trial for crimes against the Chihuahuan people and held responsible for the crimes of your government."

"Now wait just a minute…" Ned tried to interrupt. "I'm not a representative of the United States."

"Shut up," the man continued. "You are an official aide to United States Senator Michael Andreaz, and as such, will be treated as a representative of the United States Government."

How, Ned wondered, did these men know who he was? It was really too early for Jack to have started talking.

After the man left, Ned tried talking to the guard, but was almost completely ignored. The guard would look at him, but didn't seem to understand what Ned was saying. When he switched to Spanish, the guard didn't look quite as confused, but he still wouldn't respond, except to occasionally say "cállate," or "shut up" in Spanish.

***

A short time later, a woman dressed like the guards came in with two bottles of water and a burrito. A girl, thought Ned. She doesn't look old enough to be working with these men, or as worldly as she'd need to be. Why is she bringing me food?

Why is anyone bringing me food for that matter?

The guard looked at her questioningly.

"Food for the prisoner," she said in Spanish. She then held out a bottle of water for the guard and he took it and nodded. He didn't say anything else to her, but gave her an awful leer. Then, she headed toward the cell.

"Take these," she said to Ned in English. "I might be able to help you, but I can't talk for long."

"What?"

"I can help you get out. Maybe. But you have to help me too."

"How can I help you?"

"You have to take me with you, out of Juárez."

"Now wait."

"No, there's no time. Will you help me?"

Ned looked at her, trying to figure out if he could trust her, and even if he could, would she be a reliable asset. His indecision must have been apparent, as her dark eyes looked straight into Ned's.

"And I could do other things for you too." Suddenly, this girl didn't look nearly as young or as innocent as she had a moment ago.

"No, it's not that." Ned hesitated again. "How do I know I can trust you?"

"How can you trust anyone? Do you want my help?"

Ned thought quickly. Better not to limit his options.

"Okay, we'll take you back with us. Can you help my friend too?"

"Your friend?"

"Yes," replied Ned. "The man I came in with."

"I don't think he will need my help."

"What does that mean?"

"I have to go," she whispered. "I'll be back later tonight, if they haven't yet killed you."

Chapter Thirteen

The burrito had been warm and was filled with beans and rice. Ned didn't know when the next time he might eat was, so he ate it, and drank the bottle of water.

It was nearly an hour before two men in uniform arrived and removed Ned from the cell. He was trying to keep track of how many there were altogether, but he wasn't sure if these two men were the same who had originally brought him here. It was still possible that this was a relatively small operation. Together with the man that had been guarding him in his cell, the two men took Ned down some corridors and into a large room on the other side of the warehouse.

This new room was much bigger than the room Ned had been held in. Almost cavernous, it looked like it took up nearly half the warehouse. It was also far more finished.

The walls had been painted, and even the floor was roughly carpeted. It was certainly dark outside by now, but it was as bright as day in here. As Ned saw the hundreds of men in uniform sitting on benches filling most of the room, he stopped counting. This was definitely not a small operation.

It appeared that a makeshift courtroom had been set up in this large hall, with the soldiers as the courtroom gallery. There were twelve men in uniform seated as a jury. The man who had informed him earlier in his cell that he was to be put on trial was standing near the bench like a court officer. Seated at the prosecution table, and once again wearing a tie, was Jack Stuart.

Chapter Fourteen

"What the hell is going on Jack?" Ned asked as he was being seated at the defense table.

"Yeah buddy, I'd hoped to have more time to get you ready for this, but my associates aren't really the patient kind. They've been waiting for a chance like this for a long time."

"Your associates Jack? Are you saying that you've been working with these Mexican insurgents this whole time?"

"Pretty much." Jack looked slightly more pleased with himself than usual. "I was planning on waiting in El Paso with you all until tomorrow, but your little spy mission gave me the perfect opportunity to come back early. We've got big plans, Ned, and while you're certainly not a part of all of them, you'll surely come in handy here."

"And if I don't cooperate?"

"Well, I could just have you summarily executed. But come on, play along. You might live a few days longer. And if you don't cooperate, you'll still be helping us out. Even if you're bound and gagged, sitting at that table, I can still make my case. And a man staying silent at his own trial never guaranteed a not guilty verdict. It certainly won't go that way today."

"All rise for the honorable Gabriel Sanchez," the court officer shouted. The noise in the room died down and a man wearing a black robe entered from a door to what looked like a closet, and sat down at the bench.

"Court is now in session." The judge banged his gavel on the bench. "The defendant stands accused of multiple crimes." Every word that he said seemed both unfamiliar to the man and well practiced, as if he had been rehearsing but had never actually sat as a judge before. This was definitely a performance, but for what? It was then that Ned noticed the small cameras set up around the room. Not studio quality, but even a small camera could shoot high definition video. This also explained why the proceedings were being held in English. This propaganda piece wasn't only being made for supporters of this group's cause, but to embarrass the United States at home.

"Ned Albrecht," The Judge boomed. "There are a host of crimes by your government far too numerous to list here. They will be held for prosecution at a future date. Today, you stand accused, on behalf of your government, the United States of America, of stealing Chihuahuan land, terrorizing the Chihuahuan people, and illegally regulating the flow of water into the city of Ciudad Juárez. How do you plead?"

Ned wasn't sure what he wanted to do. He could be belligerent, but that would get him bound, gagged, and eventually shot; he could stick to name, rank, and serial number, which would also get him shot; or he could play along and maybe live a few days longer, like Jack suggested. Revealing any sensitive information was completely out of the question, but this wasn't an interrogation, this was a kangaroo court. They wanted a circus, and Jack was right, they'd get a good show no matter what Ned did.

"How do you plead?" The judge didn't look happy that he had to repeat himself.

Ned looked across the aisle to Jack. "I don't suppose if I plead guilty we can end this early?" Ned asked quietly.

"Not a chance," replied Jack.

"Mister Albrecht," the Judge shouted.

"Not guilty, your honor," Ned pleaded. "Not guilty."

"Your honor," Jack stood up and addressed the Judge. "I now call to the stand, the defendant, Ned Albrecht."

Chapter Fifteen

Ned was taken to the witness stand and sworn in. Jack approached him with his ever friendly smile on display.

"Would the witness like to make a statement?" Jack asked.

"Yes I would," said Ned. "I want to make it clear that although I will cooperate with these proceedings, I do not recognize the authority of this court in general, or in its right to hold me responsible for the crimes of a sovereign government."

"So noted. Anything else?"

Ned shook his head. He didn't really see the point of going on. Anything he said that might persuade someone watching would almost certainly be edited out later.

"As to the first count, stealing Chihuahuan land. Isn't

it true that in 1836 Texas declared its independence from Mexico and forced General Antonio López de Santa Anna to sign papers that granted such independence?"

"Well," said Ned. "It is true that they declared independence, and it's also true that papers were signed by Santa Anna. Historians disagree on whether or not these papers actually legitimized Texas' independence, or that Santa Anna was forced to sign. You might argue that failing to win the battle against the Texians is what forced Santa Anna to recognize Texas' independence."

"And isn't it further true that some of the lands that Texas claimed upon its independence belonged to the Free and Sovereign State of Chihuahua?"

"I believe that is correct."

"And when the United States Government annexed Texas in 1845, didn't they proceed to fight a war with the Mexican Government to protect those lands and do they not continue to hold these lands today."

"While maybe a little overly simplified, yes, I think that's true."

"Gentlemen of the jury," Jack spun around and addressed the jury directly. "I put it to you that this land was illegally seized and has been illegally held for nearly two hundred years." A large murmur ran through the crowd of people in the gallery.

"Objection," said Ned to the judge. "The prosecution is testifying."

The Judge looked at Ned, then to Jack.

"You don't have any right to object," said Jack. "In this court, it is the prosecution's job to testify. Now do you have anything else to add?"

"Only that if you continue to follow that line of logic, Mexico stole the land from Spain, Spain stole it from the Apache, and the Apache stole it from even earlier Native populations."

"Exactly," Jack shot back. "And as descendents of the original native inhabitants of this land, the people of the Free and Sovereign State of Chihuahua are the rightful heirs to any claim on this land, as well as that stolen by the United States Government."

Ned thought that he could make a decent argument that most of the people living in modern day Chihuahua were not actually descended from the pre-Apache native inhabitants, but that could anger the room and reveal him as apathetic toward their cause. Regardless, Jack didn't give him the chance to argue any further.

"Now for the second count," Jack continued. "Terrorizing the Chihuahuan people. Isn't it true that for the last six months, the United States Government has been sending four hundred deportees into Juárez daily, and isn't it further true that there has been a virtual trade embargo with the city during that time."

"Yes," said Ned. "That is true."

"Gentlemen of the jury, I put it to you that the United States Government has committed these actions without any thought or care as to how it would affect the stability of Ciudad

Juárez or the State of Chihuahua, causing the economy to crash and the murder rate to skyrocket. This caused not only impoverishment, but also the starvation and terrorization of its citizens."

"Is there anything you would like to add?" Jack had turned back around to address Ned.

"Not if I can't object to your so-called testimony."

"Very well. Next Question." Jack began to walk slowly about the courtroom area. "Do you have any justification for this mass deportation scheme? A scheme which, I will remind the jury, was not approved of by the Free and Sovereign State of Chihuahua."

"The plan was approved by the Mexican Federal Government, which has jurisdiction over Chihuahua's international affairs."

"That agreement was forced upon the powerless Mexican government by its United States masters in Washington, DC. And it's beside the point. But do tell the court what led to this deportation scheme, and if you have any justification for it."

"Well, some people say that the current immigration problems date back to 2015 and the steady increase in illegal immigration, especially the unaccompanied minors from several Central and South American countries, as well as the executive orders and congressional action that followed over the next several years. Others trace it back to the immigration reform legislation passed back in 1986."

"We don't need a history lesson," said Jack. "Is there any justification for the mass deportation of an entire people from the United States into the Free and Sovereign State of Chihuahua?"

"It isn't an entire people, and not all of them are being deported into Chihuahua."

"Again, not the point. Answer the question." Jack looked like he might be losing his patience. "Is there any justification?"

"Only that the United States is a nation of laws, and that people entering and residing in the country without authorization is a violation of those laws."

"Once again," Jack said to the jury. "We see the United States accusing everyone of Mexican origin of being a criminal."

"That's not what I said."

"But that's what you meant," Jack said to Ned. Then he turned to the jury. "You see my friends. This man continues to deny his bigoted attitude, even as he admits there was no reasonable justification for the deportation, or the undue hardship it has put upon the State of Chihuahua."

"Now to the final count," accused Jack. "Illegally regulating the flow of water into the city of Ciudad Juárez."

"Not that this court recognizes the 1906 Rio Grande water rights treaty, but didn't this treaty guarantee water be diverted into Ciudad Juárez."

"To be delivered to the Acequia Madre Canal I believe, yes."

After the first two counts, this one seemed a bit more specific to Ned. Before starting work for the senator, he had never even heard of the 1906 treaty, but water rights between Texas and Mexico were always an important political issue.

"And how much water was supposed to go to the canal, exactly?"

"I believe it was 60,000 acre feet annually, except in times of drought."

"Except in times of drought, I see. Does that explain why, for the last several years, the water flowing into the Madre Canal has been reduced to barely a trickle?"

"I wouldn't describe it as a trickle, but yes, the water has been reduced."

"And where exactly is the water reduced? Is it done at the international dam where both countries could monitor the diversion?"

"No."

"In fact," Jack continued. "The diversion is done at a dam that the United States built in 1938 to make sure that Mexico didn't take too much water. Isn't that right?"

"That is, more or less correct."

"You see my friends," Jack was once again addressing the jury. "Another example of how the Americans paint all Mexicans as criminals. Not even trusting us not to steal their water."

"Let's get back to this water reduction, Mr. Albrecht. How do we know that you aren't in fact taking more water than you should? How do we know you're dividing it fairly? We only have your word to take."

"How do you know it's not being divided fairly?"

questioned Ned. "Take my word for it. There's a drought."

"How do you explain that the American farms in the El Paso Valley are still producing crops, while nearly all of the farms on the Chihuahuan side are dead and dry?"

"It's possible that they have better water management."

"And it's possible that the American dam is giving them more water than it should."

"Gentlemen of the jury. I submit to you that the United States Government is stealing the water that rightfully belongs to the people of Chihuahua. I urge you to find Mr. Ned Albrecht, on behalf of the United States Government, guilty of this water theft, the theft of Chihuahuan lands, and of terrorism."

"The jury will now deliberate," the judge said.

"What about my defense?" asked Ned.

"Now don't go crying about it." Jack smiled. "You had every opportunity to defend your country."

The jury didn't leave the room. They just huddled together for a moment, and then were quiet.

"Has the jury reached a verdict?" the judge asked.

"We have your honor." One juror stood up as he spoke. "On all three counts your honor, we find him guilty."

Chapter Sixteen

Ned was brought back to his cell where his new friend, the guard, was once again waiting for him.

It was only a few minutes before Jack entered the room. He spoke a few words to the guard, the guard left, and Ned and Jack were left alone together.

"You'll be sentenced tomorrow," said Jack. "Aren't you glad you cooperated? You get to live another night."

"Just one?"

"We'll see. You didn't make it as easy out there as I would've liked, but you played your part. Anyway, you're a political prisoner now. You might be more valuable in a trade."

"Why are you here, Jack? Shouldn't you be editing out all the bad parts of that mock trial?" Ned couldn't seem to hide the disgust in his voice.

"Don't worry," replied Jack. "That work is being done. And there are no bad parts, only parts that are unnecessary for our cause."

"Your cause?" Ned was incredulous. "You know, you really don't seem like the type of guy to get caught up in a revolutionary army. What happened Jack, and where's the Mexican government in all this? I've been wondering that since we got here."

"The Mexican government's practically abandoned this city. There weren't even fifty federales here before tonight, and when I heard about the mass deportation, I decided it was time to put my plan into action. I ordered the Liberation Army forces to assault the border compound this afternoon. It was a bloodbath, for them. And to be honest," Jack smiled at Ned. "I'm not really with these guys. They're just a means to an end."

"Means to an end? Jack, what end could justify this?"

"While it's true," Jack was almost whispering. "That I don't really care about Chihuahuan independence, I would love to see the State of Texas throw off the yolk of the United States."

Ned was dumbfounded. He didn't understand what Jack could be thinking. He didn't seem insane, but.

"I can tell you don't understand. That's not surprising." Jack looked like he was mulling something over. "I won't tell you all my plans, but I will tell you this. With what I have in the works, Texas is going to have to form some kind of response. But do you think the boys in Washington are going to do anything. Not that senator you work for. Not that candy-ass president we have. Texas is going to have to go it alone. The way it should be."

Ned had to reevaluate his thinking on Jack. These were definitely not the actions of a sane man.

"But maybe I've said too much," said Jack. "Maybe you will have to die tomorrow."

Chapter Seventeen

Ned wasn't really trying to sleep when his next visitor arrived. Even so, he was lying on the cot in his cell with his eyes closed. It was nearing midnight, but he knew he was too restless to sleep. He wasn't even sure that sleep would be a good idea. Then the door opened and Ned looked over. It was the girl from earlier. This time, she was carrying only the two bottles of water.

As earlier, she held out the first bottle of water for the guard.

"Gracias," said the guard.

"De nada," the girl replied with a pretty smile. Then, from out of nowhere, she had a knife, and had stabbed the guard in his lower chest. The guard looked dumbfounded. He dropped the bottle of water and looked down. It looked like he was trying to speak, but had no wind.

Maybe she got him in the lung, thought Ned. By this time, he had jumped off the cot and was standing at the metal bars, still out of reach of the action.

The guard had grabbed the girl's right arm, and was pushing her as he staggered forward a couple of steps, until he fell. He landed with his head on her chest, and while it looked like he was still trying to struggle, she quickly pushed him off of her and grabbed his keys.

She opened the cell door and, as Ned was rushing out, she said, "No, we go this way." She went into the cell, took her still bloody knife, and started cutting into the drywall. Had Ned seen her remove the knife from the guard? He couldn't remember. He also hadn't noticed her taking the guard's gun, but there it was strapped over her shoulder.

"Did you really have to kill the guard?" asked Ned.

"Anything else would have made too much noise. Here, you finish." She handed the knife to Ned and he could see she was exhausted.

"Besides," she said. "He's not the first man I've killed, and he probably won't be the last."

"I'll keep that in mind," said Ned as he kept scoring into the wall.

"I'm Ned, by the way, even though you probably already know that. What's your name?"

"You can call me Lisa." she said.

"Lisa's not a very Spanish sounding name."

"My full name is Felisa Margarita Madero Valdés. Is that

Mexican sounding enough for you? But I like Lisa."

"Okay, you like Lisa. I've got it. So Lisa, is there any way we can get a hold of those courtroom recordings they made?"

She thought for a moment. "It might be possible. But is it really that important? It's just a propaganda piece. Is your embarrassment really worth risking our lives?"

"Probably not," replied Ned. Exactly how much risk are we talking about?"

"The room isn't far, but Manuel, the video technician, will be in there, and maybe a guard."

"You have a video technician?"

"Of course," she said. "He went to the University in Austin."

By this time, Ned had made a hole big enough to get his hands through and had proceeded to break off large pieces of drywall as quietly as he could. Once the hole was big enough to step through, Ned found that they were in another room the same size, but this one was almost completely empty. Lisa was removing her pants and bloody shirt to reveal jeans and a more normal looking shirt underneath. She grabbed a jacket that was sitting on the floor, tossed her hair, and suddenly, didn't look at all like she had just killed a man.

"Through the door there, there's a hallway." Lisa motioned to the only door in the room. "To the left is an exit, or we go right to find the video."

Chapter Eighteen

Ned only thought it was slightly reckless to look for the video. Lisa was right that they didn't really need it, but Ned hated the idea of being used in their propaganda piece. And there was also the issue of not really wanting his face known the world over for anything, even if he wasn't planning on doing any covert work in the future.

Fortunately, the warehouse halls seemed completely deserted, and there was only one guard with the video technician. The threat of a gunshot was enough to keep the two men quiet, and they were both soon tied to chairs and gagged. Ned expected to have to destroy several computers, as well as the cameras that had been in the courtroom, but there was only one laptop, and the cameras were not there. Manuel, the video tech, said that the three memory cards in the room were the three from the cameras, so Ned pocketed those, as well as the storage drive that he removed from the computer. After that, Ned and Lisa followed the halls back to the exit and into the night.

***

It was dark outside, but there were street lights in the area, so it wasn't completely black. Even if it had been daylight, Ned wasn't sure he would have recognized the street. There were several people lying down on the pavement, mostly in groups.

"Is it like this every night?" He asked his new companion. "Or are these the people that arrived today?"

"I try not to be out this late, but this doesn't look normal," she replied.

"Where to now?" asked Ned.

"I know a place near the border crossing where we can stay tonight," she answered. "But you better have a way to get us across. That's why I broke you out."

"I have a way, but I'm going to need a phone." Ned suddenly remembered that he was supposed to talk to General Everley's contact in Juárez. Ned had the address and phone number, but Jack had it too. The contact might already be compromised. "Can you get me to a phone?"

"The phones are out here, just like in El Paso," she said.

"But you have power here," said Ned.

"Yes, but to make sure the phones in El Paso couldn't get a signal, we had to take out the towers on this side of the border too."

Ned was disappointed. The only way to get a message to General Everley's contact now was to go in person.

"Do you know how far the 1600 block of Calle Rodolfo Ogarrio is?" asked Ned.

"It's not too far from here. Do we need to go there?"

"I need to deliver a message before we can head back."

"All right, we'll turn right at the next block, but we can't take too long, they might already be looking for us after that stunt we pulled with the video rescue."

"So what's the story with you anyway?" asked Ned. "Your English is perfect, and Lisa's not an extremely common Mexican nickname."

"I already told you, my name is…"

"Yes I know. Felisa Margarita, but why Lisa as a nickname?"

"So you want my entire life story now?" She paused, then continued. "I went to private schools in El Paso from the time that I was little. A girl in the first grade wanted to call me Lisa, and it just stuck. And before you get all politically correct about staying true to my Mexican heritage, it was another Mexican girl that called me Lisa."

"No, I was just curious. I actually like Lisa."

"Well," she paused, like she was getting ready for another argument. But then she finished quietly. "Good."

There were plenty of people on the streets. As they moved farther away from the warehouses and nearer downtown, there were fewer people making camps, and more people wandering around. It looked like all the bars were open for anyone who wanted to find a drink to bring them cheer or to drown their sorrows. Ned thought it might get ugly around closing time, but then decided that closing time wasn't likely to happen in this mostly lawless town. Not unless the liberation army was enforcing the local law, which, he expected, was pretty unlikely.

"I can't believe all these people are out," said Lisa. "Normally the streets would be empty at this time of night. Too dangerous."

"It must be the deportees," said Ned. "A sudden population increase of fourteen thousand is bound to cause at least a temporary change in the city's nightlife."

"Fourteen thousand?" That number always seemed to incite this kind of shocked response. "What were you thinking?"

"It wasn't exactly my idea," replied Ned.

"Of course not. Blame everything on the bureaucrats, right?"

The question seemed rhetorical, so Ned let it lie.

The crowd had thinned out almost completely by the time they arrived at the address of General Everley's contact. It was a small adobe looking house with a short wall around the property, and while there were mostly single family homes on the block, the neighborhood didn't have a very residential feeling to it.

Ned knocked on the door, waited, and then knocked again.

"Who is it?" a voice shouted from the other side of the

door.

"My name is Ned. A friend from El Paso sent me. He told me to ask you about your dachshund."

The door opened and a man rushed Ned and Lisa inside.

"Cesar?" Ned asked.

"Yes. What are you doing here?" His English was not as good as Lisa's but it was passable.

"We, the man I crossed the border with and I, we were supposed to reestablish contact with you after the blackout. Unfortunately, that man is working with the insurgents here in Juárez. Your cover is burned."

"My cover? I don't have a cover. This is my life."

"Regardless, he could be on his way now. You have to get out. Will you come with us, or, do you have a place to go?"

"Come with you? No. I have a family. But I do have a place to go. Give me a minute." Cesar proceeded to wake his wife and instruct her to pack the essentials and get the car ready. Several minutes later, he returned to Ned and Lisa.

"I don't suppose you have any cash for me?" Cesar asked.

"I'm afraid not," replied Ned. "But if you want to tell me where you're going, I might be able to arrange something. I do have to ask. Do you know anything about the missile attack in El Paso or the insurgent army here in Juárez?"

"The Chihuahuan Liberation Army," said Cesar. "Yes, they've been building their ranks for some time. They probably number in the hundreds now."

"Thousands." The previously silent Lisa spoke up for the first time since entering the house.

"I didn't expect that they had the resources for any kind of missile attack," Cesar continued. "But I wouldn't be surprised if it was them."

"Oh, it was definitely them," said Lisa.

"Really?" asked Cesar. "And how exactly would you know that?" He looked at her more closely. "Didn't you used to work at that burrito café?"

"I just have one of those faces," she said. "And I would know about the army, because I was with them."

Ned was really wishing that Lisa wasn't sharing information with Cesar so freely.

"It looks like your girlfriend here knows more about it than I do. I better get back to my packing. It's time for you to leave."

"Wait," said Ned. "One more thing, do you know where I could find a working telephone?"

"I heard someone say earlier today that some of the old land line phones were still working. A few of the older residents in town still have them, and some businesses, but I don't know where you could find one to use at this time of night."

"Thank you, we'll go now. You should hurry."

"We will. But we can't leave everything behind."

Cesar walked them to the door, and as they walked away, Ned could hear the door lock behind them.

Chapter Nineteen

Much to Lisa's dismay, Ned had insisted that they watch the house until Cesar's family left. They took up an inconspicuous spot that had a view of both the front of Cesar's house, as well as the back access. About twenty minutes after they left, they saw Cesar carrying several bags out to the car. Shortly after, he and his wife carried several more bags and a baby seat out of the house and drove away.

"All right," said Ned as he started walking. "Let's get going."

"It's about time," replied Lisa. "It's nearly five kilometers."

"Listen, I know it doesn't seem important, but he helped us..."

"He didn't help us." Lisa interrupted.

"Let me rephrase that." Ned thought for a moment. "He

risked his life by helping my government, and if Jack had come here looking for us, and ended up killing him, that would have been a disservice to him on my part."

"Whatever," she said, as she led Ned east down the dark streets.

"So listen. I want you to tell me what you know about that army you were a part of. How did you get mixed up with them anyway?"

"My life story again," she said. "How exactly is this important?"

"Well, it seems like you wanted to get out of there, but I have no idea about your motives. It would help me understand you if I understood why you wanted to leave and why you were there in the first place."

"My brother got involved with the group after our parents were murdered," Lisa explained. "He told me I should get in too. I was always apprehensive, but life in Juárez was dangerous, and they offered some stability. They would feed and clothe you, protect you, and Chihuahuan independence didn't seem like such a bad idea at first. Also, you hear stories about women holding power in revolutionary armies, so I was optimistic at the beginning. But while I was given some authority, the leaders basically treated me like a child. Not everyone was terrible to me, but it wasn't a good life. As I spent more time with the group, I saw the way that they treated the people who wouldn't join. They were worse than the drug cartels, openly killing people in the street. Now I think they actually control the cartels. They try to keep secret how large the army's influence has grown, but I hear a lot of rumors."

"What kind of rumors?" asked Ned.

"That they control the drug cartels. That they have a base set up in Chihuahua City. That they have the backing of a lot of the upright and wealthy Chihuahuan citizens, as well as some Americans."

"Are these rumors true?"

"It's difficult to say how true. There's certainly influence over the drug cartels, they have some kind of base in Chihuahua City, and they must have financial backing. You know that they have help from your American friend."

Ned knew this much was true. He still couldn't believe Jack's reasoning for supporting their cause.

"Anyway," Lisa continued. "I wanted out of that place, especially now with this talk about invading El Paso…"

"What?" Ned interrupted. "Invading El Paso? Is this another rumor?"

"No," she said. "Not a rumor. They're making plans."

"When is this supposed to happen, and why didn't you tell me this sooner?"

"We've been busy," said Lisa. "And I don't know exactly when it's supposed to happen. It's still secret, and I'm not even sure they know yet. They seem to be waiting for something. But it's very soon. Probably before power can be restored in El Paso, so the next couple of days. The blackout was the first step in their plan."

"This doesn't make any sense. Why would they invade El

Paso? What do they have to gain? What can they accomplish?"

"I don't have all the answers," answered Lisa. "I think it sounds crazy too. You heard them at the trial. They have unrealistic issues with the United States. Stealing land, stealing water, terrorism. Well, the water rights might be a legitimate claim, and your country certainly could have found a better way to deal with its migrant worker problem, but it seems ludicrous to go to war about it. Anyway, the trial was also a part of the plan to justify the invasion."

"Do you think they have enough people to make any kind of invasion work?" asked Ned.

"They number in the thousands now, and they recruit daily, often from the deportees you send across, and you just sent them fourteen thousand more."

"Again, not my decision."

"Your government," Lisa replied. "Anyway, they definitely have enough people to storm the border, and they're planning to encourage the Juárez residents to cross into El Paso and occupy the city. That shouldn't be too hard because much of El Paso has been abandoned, and Juárez is extremely overcrowded. As far as holding the city against the American army, they probably couldn't do that, but your friend Jack Stuart has assured us that the United States Government would lack the resolve to take back the city after it was occupied."

The more Lisa talked, the more it made sense to Ned, especially after what Jack had told him about provoking a response from Texas. He was suddenly very impatient. The twenty minutes waiting for Cesar's family to go had been a waste of time. He was now even questioning whether or not he should have even contacted Cesar in the first place. He needed to get back to El Paso immediately, or at the very least find a phone. Ned knew that the situation at the border wouldn't allow them to cross overnight.

"Where can we find a phone?" asked Ned.

"I have an idea about that, but it won't work until morning."

"What's the idea?"

"The place where we're going to. There's a hotel next door. I can pay to use their phone in the morning."

"Why not now?"

"No one's going to open up their door for us now, except for maybe those bars downtown, but they probably don't even have land line phones. They're not exactly licensed establishments."

"We could break in," said Ned. "Or force our way in."

"No," said Lisa. "If the hotel owner doesn't kill us, we might have to kill him. Even if I was ready to kill an innocent man, it would draw too much attention." She looked at Ned emphatically. "We wait until morning."

Chapter Twenty

They arrived at the address. It looked like a small warehouse to Ned. Lisa used a remote device that she retrieved from her pocket to open an automated garage door. Inside the garage area, Ned could see that the warehouse façade was built around the exterior of a house and encompassed what was once the entire yard. Inside, there was the old front of the home.

"So, what is this place anyway?" asked Ned.

"It is the home that belonged to a friend of my father. When he left for Mexico City, he asked me to take care of it for him."

"Did you think about getting out of the city when he left?"

"Not really," replied Lisa. "I wanted to make sure that my

family's business was taken care of."

"Your family's business?"

"Yes. We had a restaurant just north of downtown. I ran it for three months last year until the crime became overwhelming. We reopened it as kind of a cantina for the army officers. I was still more or less running the place, but it's not like it used to be. My father didn't serve alcohol because he didn't like dealing with drunken customers. Now, that's all there is in there."

They went through the front door of the house. Lisa turned on a light and Ned could see that it looked like a regular home.

"It looks like he thought he was coming back," said Ned.

"He still may, but things look a lot more uncertain now than they did when he left. Either way, he'll be okay."

"How can you be so certain?" asked Ned.

"He has money," Lisa replied.

"Your family had money too."

"My family ran a successful business. Señor Menendez was sitting on a fortune. I think the only reason he stayed as long as he did was because he grew up here. Crime waves have come and gone in Juárez, but this time was different. You can see the way he built the house up into a fortress. You have to take extreme measures if you want to try and live a normal life in this city today. And in the end, he still left. I would have gone too if I had that kind of money. But moving out of Juárez would have meant starting over for me. I probably should have, but I wanted to make the restaurant work, and so did my brother. I thought we had each other to lean on. I suppose we did for a while."

"What happened to your brother?" asked Ned.

"He's still with the liberation army."

"Will they punish him because you left?"

"I don't think so. He abandoned me months ago anyway. I tried to tell him that I wanted to get out, but he wouldn't help me. Said it would look bad for him if I left. If they punish him now, he deserves what he gets."

"What time can we make that phone call tomorrow?"

"Not before seven." Lisa replied.

"How about six?" asked Ned.

"Fine, we'll try at six. It should be light out by then anyway."

She then pointed down a short hallway to a door. "I'm sleeping in that room. There are two more bedrooms on the other side of the house." She motioned in the other direction with her other hand.

"Goodnight," she said as she walked into the room and closed the door behind her.

Ned said goodnight through the closed door and proceeded to find his own bed for the night. There was an alarm clock in the room, which said that it was after two in the morning. He set the alarm for five-thirty, and after lying in bed for nearly an hour, he finally fell asleep.

It was at five o'clock that he awoke from the sound of the explosion.

Chapter Twenty-One

The explosion didn't just sound loud. It shook the ground. Ned was up and pounding on Lisa's door before she was out of bed.

"What is it?" Lisa shouted from inside the room.

"You didn't hear that?"

"I heard it. What was it?"

"I don't know, but we have to go."

Lisa came out of the room a minute later, dressed and with her hair in a ponytail. Ned figured that she had also slept in her clothes, just in case.

"Are you ready?" asked Ned.

"No, I need a few minutes."

"Hurry," said Ned. "I'm going to take a peek outside."

Ned went outside of the house and opened the garage

door in the exterior wall. The street still looked empty. Someone saw the door open and asked loudly in Spanish what was going on. Ned replied that he didn't know, and closed the garage door again.

By the time he got back inside, Lisa was eating stale crackers that she found in the cupboard.

"Bring those," said Ned. "We can eat them on the way. We need to get going."

"Going where? Don't you still want to find a phone?"

"If we can, but I need to find out what that explosion was."

"It might have been a car explosion. They're not that uncommon here."

"You must have been sleeping pretty hard. It sounded like it was far away, but with the way the ground shook, it must have been huge."

"So what do you want to do?"

"We'll check next door for the phone, then we'll head to the border to see if we can find out anything."

They left the house and walked to the hotel. The streets still seemed mostly empty, but there were now a few people walking around. Ned hit the buzzer and banged on the door at the hotel. A voice on the other end of an intercom told them to go away or get shot.

As they walked to the border, they continued to see larger groups of people gathered together. Ned stopped and asked almost every group they passed if they knew about the explosion. Nobody knew, but many had theories, from cars exploding to a second missile attack on El Paso. There was also talk about gunfire closer to the border.

Ned was leading Lisa to the deportation port where he and Jack had initially entered into Juárez. He thought that maybe he could convince the border guard to let them cross. As they approached the buildings, he could see that the border station was occupied by men wearing the uniforms of the Chihuahuan Liberation Army.

Chapter Twenty-Two

Ned and Lisa had backed up to a point where they were out of sight of the border patrol station and joined a group of people who had huddled together. Again, none of them seemed to know what was going on.

It wasn't long before several pickup trucks pulled out of the border patrol station. It looked like they were carrying giant theater speakers in the back.

"People of Juárez," a pre-recorded voice boomed from the truck in Spanish. "The Chihuahuan Liberation Army has taken control of the border into El Paso. El Paso is completely abandoned, and there are homes sitting empty for everyone. All residents with no place to stay should cross the border into El Paso and claim an abandoned home."

The message began to repeat. Ned could hear an echo

begin as more than one truck was playing the message as they drove off in different directions. Ned wondered how long it would take these trucks to cover the city, but quickly decided that there must be other trucks starting from other locations.

"What do you think?" asked Lisa. "Should we go into El Paso?"

"It's not a bad idea, but I don't want to be the first ones through, and it's possible they'll be looking for us. Do you think any of the soldiers there will recognize you?"

"It's possible, especially if they're looking for us. Maybe you're right, and we should wait."

They walked a little farther from the border patrol station and waited. It was only about fifteen minutes before there was a large crowd of people walking toward the border.

"Okay," said Ned. "I think now's the time to go."

As they walked closer to the border, Ned could see that the drawbridge doors were open and that the Chihuahuan soldiers did indeed control both sides of the border. As a matter of fact, Ned thought they looked as well organized as the American soldiers had when he first arrived in Juárez. There were still bodies strewn about, but the Chihuahuan soldiers were already clearing the area. Ned could tell by the uniforms that there were both American and Chihuahuan soldiers among the dead.

Ned and Lisa kept their heads down and continued to approach the border crossing without speaking. The Chihuahuan soldiers were telling the people crossing the bridge that the fighting was over, and that they would be safe in El Paso, as long as they avoided the American encampments. They were directing the people east and west. Ned could see that to the north there were more bodies, and that the American soldiers had retreated and established a new stronghold at the edge of the green zone, not even a half a mile away.

"The Americans are still pretty close," said Lisa. "Are we safe here?"

"Probably safe from standard rifle fire, but certainly not from a decent sniper. And if they decided to bring in tanks or air support, there's no way the Chihuahuans could hold the border. Still, like you suggested earlier, it's likely they won't want the bad publicity that would come from slaughtering Mexican civilians."

"Come on," continued Ned. "We're heading east. We need to get into the green zone, and I know a place where we can cross."

"So Lisa?" asked Ned. "Were those Mexican flags that the Chihuahuans were flying at the border crossing? They were the same ones they were using at the trial, but they didn't look quite right."

"It's the Chihuahuan Liberation Army flag. It has the green, white and red stripes of the Mexican flag, but uses the seal of Chihuahua in the middle instead of the Mexican coat of arms."

"I see," said Ned. "Isn't there usually an eagle with a snake?"

"Yes. It's an old Aztec symbol of a golden eagle

devouring a snake. I don't know what it originally meant, but today people look at it as Mexico, represented by the eagle, destroying the evil snake."

"That's interesting," said Ned. "I've always thought of the United States as an eagle, but not Mexico." Ned paused for a moment. "A bald eagle and a golden eagle."

"And now they're fighting," said Lisa.

"Like dueling eagles."

Chapter Twenty-Three

Most of the people from Juárez who had crossed the border with Ned and Lisa were heading east along the highway that ran parallel to the Rio Grande river basin, which was also the border with Juárez. Ned had decided to stay with the crowd because they were mainly heading in the right direction and staying with the group would continue to keep them from being more readily noticed.

As they walked, Ned could see that there were Chihuahuan soldiers cutting the fence posts that lined either side of the river with some kind of portable reciprocating saws.

"Was that part of the plan?" asked Ned.

Lisa looked over to where the men were working. "Not that I knew of, but it only makes sense that they would want to make it easier for the people to come into El Paso since civilian occupation is the major reason they believe the United States won't take back the city."

The men were making quick work of the fences. The fence panels were quickly falling over, and the soldiers were leaving them where they lay.

"Let's take a closer look," said Ned.

They tried to look inconspicuous as they separated from the crowd and moved closer to the border fences. The chain-link fence nearer to them was still up, but they could see through it easily, and the soldiers didn't seem to take any notice of them.

"Do you see that?" asked Lisa.

"What?"

"The canal is empty."

Ned looked down at the concrete lined basin. It was wet, as if there had recently been water in it, but there was no water flowing.

"I don't understand," said Ned. "Isn't the Rio Grande always dry along here?"

"Yes," replied Lisa. "It's like an Arroyo. But that isn't the Rio Grande. That's the American Canal where most of the Rio Grande water is diverted to. It's almost always flowing."

Ned looked further away, past where the men were taking down the fences, and could see the Rio Grande river basin, which was also empty.

"What could have stopped the canal flow?" asked Ned.

"They must have diverted the water. Probably at the

American Dam. Maybe that was the explosion."

"But if they blew up the dam," said Ned. "Wouldn't there be water flowing down the riverbed?"

"I suppose you're right. Still, something's going on with the water."

"Especially after all the talk about water rights at the trial," said Ned. "This must be part of their plan."

"Maybe they diverted the water into Juárez at the International Dam."

Ned thought for a moment. "You could be right. That would actually be a convincing reason as to why they'd invade El Paso, they would have to hold the dams if they were going to maintain the water flow."

Ned and Lisa rejoined the group on the main road. As they continued to walk with the border fences on their right and the highway sound barriers on their left, Ned began to feel like he was once again on the deportation highway, being herded along a predetermined path. He knew that they needed to head north, but just the two of them breaking from the rest of the group and trying to climb over the sound barriers would draw too much attention.

They had been walking for a little more than twenty minutes when they saw a sign that read, "Fonseca Drive, one-half mile." Some people continued to walk, but the sign was causing others to become impatient and they started looking for a way to climb the wall. It wasn't impossibly high, but at six feet, it was going to be difficult for most people to scale by themselves.

"Come on," said Ned, as he held out his hands for Lisa to step on.

She stepped up, he gave her an additional push, and she was at the top and then over. Ned helped a couple of other agile looking people up and over like this before asking someone else to give him a hand. Once he was over the wall, he could see that they were in some kind of park with a street called Edna Avenue on the other side.

Heading east on Edna, they entered a residential neighborhood. It looked to be mostly abandoned with many of the houses' windows being boarded over. The people who were following them from the other side of the sound barrier began to break up as they examined the homes, looking for a place to stay. Ned imagined that if any of these homes were still occupied, there'd be trouble when the new arrivals decided to move in. Best to keep moving for now.

"Do you know this neighborhood at all?" asked Ned. We need to get to Cortez Drive. I think it's east of here, but it looks like this street doesn't go through."

"Not well," replied Lisa. "I know that Highway Sixty-Two is north of here."

"Sixty-Two is the border to the green zone," said Ned. "But we need to get to Cortez if we're going to cross over. We'll head north for now."

As they wound their way through the neighborhoods, Ned was surprised at how quiet the streets were. If there were gangs controlling the streets, it must have been too early in the morning for them to be out. They eventually found their way to Cortez Drive and headed north until they reached the wall into the green zone.

"Do you see that?" Ned motioned toward a large gate in the wall.

"Of course," replied Lisa.

"That's where we're going in."

Just then, there was the sound of a gunshot. Ned and Lisa both ran for cover.

"That was a blank warning shot," a voice over a bullhorn boomed. "Do not approach the gate or you will be fired upon."

Ned cupped his hands into a makeshift megaphone and yelled back, "I have a password."

"Say again," the loud voice boomed.

Ned tried to shout even louder. "I have a password."

There was a short pause, then, "The two of you, approach the gate slowly with your hands up."

Chapter Twenty-Four

Ned and Lisa did as the voice had ordered. They approached the gate with their hands raised above their heads. As they neared the gate, the voice spoke again.

"State your password," the voice boomed, even though Ned couldn't see anybody there.

"Mockingbird," shouted Ned.

There was no immediate response. Ned knew they would have to look it up.

"Challenge word," the voice continued. "Vienna. Please state the countersign."

"Fritzling," replied Ned.

There was another momentary wait, then a small door opened in the larger gate. A United States soldier holding a rifle was on the other side.

"Approach the door one at a time." The soldier made eye contact with Ned. "You first, then the girl. You will be searched for weapons. Do not lower your hands until the search has ended."

"I have a gun strapped over my shoulder underneath my jacket," said Ned.

"And I have a knife," Lisa added.

The soldier nodded. "So noted," he said.

The soldier backed away and Ned and Lisa went through the door. Lisa was frisked by one soldier who removed her knife while another soldier removed Ned's jacket, and then his gun.

"Sorry about all that, but we're on high alert since this morning," the soldier said. "According to your password, you're either Ned Albrecht or Jack Stuart."

"Ned Albrecht. And you need to revoke that password. Jack Stuart is no longer a friendly."

"Is that so?" the soldier looked surprised. "Well yes sir, I'll pass that on."

"Listen," said the soldier. We're pretty busy here, is there someone I can call for you?"

"If you can get me in touch with Director Rodriguez or General Everley," said Ned.

"Not directly," the soldier replied. "But we can put you on our next transport to HQ. Anyone else?"

"Captain Smith, or Private Philips."

The soldier hit a button on the radio he was wearing. "I have a Ned Albrecht here looking for Captain Smith or

Private Philips, over."

"Philips here," a voice replied on the radio. "Where is Mister Albrecht? Over."

"We're here at gate seven, over."

"Roger that, I'm on my way, over and out."

"Well then," the soldier said. "It looks like you two have a ride."

***

Private Philips arrived just a few minutes later in the same vehicle that they had driven the day before.

"Good to see you Mister Albrecht." The private jumped out of the vehicle and opened the back door. "It looks like you made a friend."

"Private Philips, this is Lisa Madero. Lisa, Private Philips."

"Miss Madero." The private tipped his hat as he held the door for Lisa. Then, speaking directly to Ned. "Mister Stuart isn't with you?"

"I'm afraid that Mister Stuart is working with the Mexican insurgents." Ned was getting into the front passenger seat. "Where are we headed Philips?"

"Jack's with the Mexicans?" There was a visible look of shock on his face. "Sorry sir, we're headed back to the Civilian Op HQ. I've been assisting Director Rodriguez there since last night."

"So we're seeing the director?"

"That's right sir," the private replied. "How could Mister Stuart be with the Mexicans?"

"Well private, that's kind of a long story, and we only have a few blocks to drive, so we better save it for later. Has anything been happening here that I should know about?"

"As you might assume sir, all hell kind of broke loose this morning when the Mexicans stormed the border."

"Do you know anything about what they're doing?"

"Only that they seem to be massing at the two dam sites, but they're taking down fences all along the border. We've completely retreated into the green zone. Casualties have been relatively low, but we lost more than a hundred men early on in the fighting. Almost everyone standing at the border was shot down. It was a well coordinated attack, and we weren't expecting it at all. By the time we thought to charge back, the border had already been lost."

Ned thought that he was pretty well informed for a private, but it must have come from working with Director Rodriguez.

"And what about that explosion?" asked Ned.

"That was at the International Dam. It went off at the same time they stormed the border. They did a pretty good job of it too. It looks like even when we take back the dam, the water's still going to be flowing down the Rio Grande for a while."

They arrived at the operational headquarters building and walked into the lobby.

The private led them to the elevator. "The soldiers that the general sent down yesterday managed to get the generator working, so there's power in the building now."

They proceeded to the Director's office.

Ned introduced Lisa to Director Rodriguez and briefly recounted the story of their capture and Jack's betrayal.

"You know," said the director. "I always thought there was something a bit off about that man."

"Well," said Ned. "Hindsight being twenty-twenty, there were some things about him that seem off to me now too, but I had no idea that he was going to betray us like that."

"No," the director replied. "You're right. I didn't see this coming either."

The satellite phone that was sitting on the director's desk started to ring. "I called the general and told him that you were on your way. He said he would call back, so this is probably him."

She picked up the phone, pressed a button on it, and held it to her ear.

"Yes general, he's here now. Would you like to talk to him? What? No? Are you certain that's necessary? All right general. I understand. Goodbye."

"Abby, what was that?" asked Ned.

"That was the general," the director replied. "He said that the only reason we've been holding the green zone as long as we have is because we've been waiting for you to return. He's now ordering the evacuation of the city and we're to retreat to Biggs Army Airfield."

"To the airfield?" asked Ned. "Does that mean they're abandoning the headquarters at Fort Bliss as well?"

Director Rodriguez looked as concerned about the situation as Ned felt. Finally she said, "It would appear so."

Chapter Twenty-Five

It was only ten o'clock in the morning, but it felt much later to Ned. What little sleep he had gotten last night wasn't good sleep, and he'd been on his feet for nearly five hours.

Once again, Ned was back inside the military transport vehicle, with Private Philips driving. Director Rodriguez and her secretary were riding in the two back seats, and Lisa had been relegated to sitting in the storage area in the back.

It took them nearly half an hour to make the trip, even though they were at the front of the mass retreat to the airfield. As they drove past the administrative section of Fort Bliss, Ned could see dozens of trucks being loaded full of filing cabinets and computers. It was such a massive amount of work, Ned had to believe that they wouldn't be going through with this unless the general believed it was absolutely necessary.

By the time they arrived at the airfield, there were already dozens of temporary shelters set up, and dozens more in the process. There were also several hangars with their bay doors wide open, and one large office building where they were to report to the general.

Ned introduced Lisa to the general and once again told the story about his night in Mexico.

"So your friend Jack's a traitor," General Everley stated. "But you say his real aim is Texan independence from the United States. It's hard for me to wrap my head around that one."

"All due respect General," said Director Rodriguez. "You're not from Texas. That attitude, while not common, is something most native Texans have run into at some point. There are definitely a significant number of people raised here who feel that Texas should not be beholden to the United States government."

"Part and parcel with 'the South shall rise again' crowd, I expect," said the general. "Yes, I ran into people like that myself growing up. Thinking that the southern states would indeed once again rise up against the federal government." The general shook his head.

"But what do we do now, General?" asked Ned. "Why have we completely abandoned the city?"

"According to satellite imagery of this morning's invasion, we believe they have more than twenty thousand soldiers. Add to that the civilian population that is flooding into El

Paso, and there's no way we have the manpower to defend the green zone. Certainly not without bringing out the heavy machinery and mowing them down, and the president isn't ready for mass casualties. We're going to be raising bulwarks around the airfield and will be holding position here for now."

"Director Rodriguez will be staying here to administrate the relocation center," the general continued. "Even after yesterday's deportation, there are still several thousand aliens being held there, and someone has to look after them as I expect they aren't going to be deported anytime soon."

"You, Mister Albrecht, are going to be on a plane to Austin before noon. Your senator boss is there and is anxious to see you, as is the governor. I'll call ahead and tell them what you've told me. Your new friend can stay here and I'll have her debriefed."

"No General, Miss Madero is coming with me. You can debrief her before I go, but I'm not going to leave her behind."

The general gave Ned an awful glare. That look told Ned that the general wasn't going to go along with this easily.

"I'll talk to Senator Andreaz about this if I have to," Ned continued. "But I'm certain he'll back me up."

The general held his stare for a moment, but then relented.

"All right Mister Albrecht," said the general. "Have it your own way."

Chapter Twenty-Six

Ned sat in on Lisa's debriefing. It wasn't the first time
that he had seen this kind of thing done, in fact, he'd gone
through it himself more than once, but he was still amazed
at the efficiency and effectiveness of the questions that were
asked by someone who was trained to do so. The additional
information that the interviewer dug out of her about
the Chihuahuan Liberation Army seemed so much more
comprehensive than what Ned had learned while talking to
her on their way out of Juárez. After the interview was over,
Lisa told Ned she hadn't even realized how much she knew,
until all the questions were asked.

After the debriefing, Ned and Lisa were both rushed to
a military plane that had been waiting for them to leave for
Austin. Unlike the plane that had flown Ned into El Paso,

which was filled with soldiers, this one was smaller, and nearly empty.

"I've only flown on a plane once before," said Lisa. "And that was to visit my aunt in California back when I was eleven."

"It probably wasn't like this plane," said Ned.

"Not at all. It was enormous, with rows and rows of seats, and every one filled. It was so crowded. My father complained about the leg room, but I was so little I didn't even notice."

"Plenty of leg room here alright," said Ned. "And there are only thirty seats. Even if it was full, it wouldn't seem crowded."

Lisa looked around. There were only three other people on the plane, but everyone had spread out so that no one was sitting together except for Ned and Lisa.

"They aren't evacuating the civilians?" asked Lisa.

"They're probably being evacuated to the airfield, but until the military starts to get a better handle on exactly what's going on with this invasion, they probably won't be arranging military transport for civilians. Of course, anyone who has a car can still drive away, but there aren't a lot of people left in El Paso who have cars that aren't supporting the military on some level, so they'll be expected to stay anyway. I expect that the only reason they chartered this flight was to send you and me back to Austin. You should feel privileged."

"I might, if they were doing it for me," said Lisa. "I was supposed to stay in El Paso, remember?"

Ned nodded quietly.

"Why do you want me in Austin with you anyway?"

"Well, I thought that the senator would want to meet with you, since a lot of the intelligence I gathered in Mexico comes from what you know."

"There has to be more than that. I'd think you wanted to sleep with me, except... I was really surprised when you argued with the general about me, because, I didn't think you liked me."

"Listen Lisa. It's not that I don't like you. It's just that I have a girlfriend, so I'm not going to have romantic feelings for you. But I do like you, and I never would have gotten out of Juárez without your help."

"So now you think you have to take care of me?"

"Sort of, but it's not that simple. When you first said that you could get me out of that jail cell, you told me that I had to take you with me, out of Juárez. Now we're out, but there's still a good chance you could get lost in the shuffle, maybe even end up with the deportees. I've seen people fall through the cracks before, and I don't want that to happen to you, especially not after our agreement in Juárez. So, it's not so much that I have to take care of you, as it is that I have a responsibility to make sure you're okay. Like that's part of the deal. Do you understand?"

"I think so," she said. "I hope that doesn't mean I'm stuck with you forever now."

"Not forever, no. But you might have to put up with me until I can get you a resident's visa."

"How long will that take?"

"If we were in Washington, I could probably push an emergency visa through in a day. It will probably take longer from Austin though."

They sat quietly for a moment. Then Lisa spoke.

"So you have a girlfriend?"

"Yes," said Ned. "Her name's Marlene. She's a reporter. I'm probably overdue to give her a call. Maybe when we land."

They sat quietly for another moment. Then Lisa spoke again.

"You said earlier that there were some people in El Paso who didn't have cars so they couldn't leave?"

"It wouldn't be easy for them," said Ned. "Not now anyway."

"I suppose the people who don't have cars are the poor," said Lisa.

"And the homeless," said Ned.

"I guess it's not only the people of Juárez that have been suffering."

"No, not only them, but many El Paso residents had a way out back when this thing started. The government had a buyout program for people whose home values had been deprecated, which was pretty much everyone who owned a home. I actually did a lot of work on that program for the senator. Renters weren't as well taken care of, but there were programs for them as well. There were even free buses that ran from El Paso to Dallas back in February for anyone who wanted to take them, so even the poor had a way out, if they had wanted to leave."

"So you took care of your own people. I suppose that's only natural. It's just sad there wasn't anyone to take care of us in Juárez."

They sat in silence for a moment before Lisa asked how long the flight would last.

"Less than an hour," answered Ned.

"Hardly enough time to sleep then."

"Go ahead and close your eyes," said Ned. "You might get forty winks."

"How long is forty winks?"

"Twenty minutes," said Ned. "That's the shortest nap I'd recommend."

"Will you close your eyes too?"

"I will."

Ned closed his eyes, but he didn't sleep.

Chapter Twenty-Seven

Ned opened his eyes when he heard the announcement from the pilot that the plane was descending. Lisa was asleep, so he gently nudged her in the arm.

"Are we there?" she asked.

"Almost," Ned replied. "I'm going to go and talk to the pilot."

There was no attendant on the plane, but there was a pilot and a co-pilot, both of whom Ned had met before the plane took off from El Paso. The cockpit door was open, so Ned asked if he could come up, and the co-pilot waved him in.

"Have we been given clearance to land?" asked Ned.

"We have," the co-pilot answered. "It looks like we've been given priority clearance because we're a military flight.

There are several commercial flights in holding patterns waiting for clearance."

"Is that unusual?" asked Ned.

"In my experience," said the pilot. "It's very unusual. The only reason I can think that there would be this many planes waiting to land is if all flights are being grounded. I asked the air traffic controllers about it, but they wouldn't confirm, not that you would expect them to."

"Anyhow," the pilot continued. "We're getting ready to touch down. You should retake your seat, unless you want to buckle in up here."

Ned made his way back to his seat and told Lisa they were getting ready to land.

***

Once the military plane had landed, Ned's phone, which had been held by the Army during his trip to Juárez, was working like it should again. In addition to several missed calls and voicemails, there were also dozens of new texts, some from the senator's office and many others that were related to his work as the senator's aide. There were only two from Marlene. The first was from last evening and said, "Where are you?" The second, from this morning, said simply, "Call me."

There was a car with a military driver waiting for them on the runway. It wasn't far from the Austin-Bergstrom airport to the State Capitol Building, but it would still take twenty to thirty minutes to make the drive.

"I better call Marlene," Ned said to Lisa. "I'm not sure when I'll get another chance."

"Okay," said Lisa, as she nodded her head.

Ned made the call, and he could hear the phone ringing on the other end.

"Hello," the voice on the other end said.

"Hey, Marlene, you wanted me to call."

"You better believe I wanted you to call. What with all the rumors about the mass deportation last night, and now the trouble on the border this morning. There's been what amounts to a media blackout down there. I was worried. You're not in El Paso, are you?"

"No, not anymore," said Ned.

"But you were in El Paso!" Marlene sounded shocked. "And you didn't tell me. I ought to come down there and smack you in the head. Where are you now?"

"Back in Austin."

"Are you coming back here?"

"I don't know yet," said Ned. "I'm going to meet with the governor and Senator Andreaz now."

"The senator's there?"

"The senator's here, yes, but I don't know if that's on the record. You'll have to confirm it somewhere else."

"Right, I'll call your office. So what were you doing in El Paso anyway? And what's going on there? There are rumors that the border was compromised but the army won't confirm anything and local communication has been cut off. We're actually getting more news out of Juárez. There's some organization I've never heard of taking credit for the trouble. The CLA?"

"The Chihuahuan Liberation Army. Come on Marlene, even if I could talk about this, I couldn't do it over the phone."

"Do you want me to fly down there?"

"No," said Ned. "Don't come to Austin. Definitely don't go to El Paso. Not that you could find a flight there."

"That's another thing," said Marlene. "It looks like they're grounding flights, and there's something going on in New Mexico too."

"What's going on in New Mexico?"

"I don't know," said Marlene. "We got notice about a half an hour ago from the local news agents about some kind of explosion, but they've gone quiet now too. Usually some kind of news filters out, even if the official channels are closed, but hardly anything's come out of El Paso, so if this is related to that…"

"Yeah," said Ned. "I don't think it'll be the same, but you're right. It could be related. Anyway, I've got to go. We're arriving at the capitol grounds now."

Chapter Twenty-Eight

There was no waiting this time as Ned and Lisa were rushed into the governor's office. Senator Andreaz was already in with the governor.

"Well there he is," said the Governor. "Mister Ned Albrecht home from the war. You know Senator, I told this boy not to be stupid by leaving the green zone, and he up and decides to leave the country instead."

"Might I remind you, Arvin," said the senator. "That your man Stuart went with him."

"Yeah," the governor replied. "And look how that turned out. That lousy no-good…"

"Mister Governor," Senator Andreaz interrupted. "Might I remind you that we have a lady present?"

"Oh, right," said the governor. "Is this the girl who got

you out of that jam in Mexico?"

"The very one," said Ned. "Might I introduce both of you gentlemen to Miss Lisa Madero?"

"Charmed," said the governor. "Now that we have the introductions out of the way, can we get down to business? Ned, your friend is going to need to wait outside."

"Of course," replied Ned. He then looked at Lisa.

"I'll wait outside," she said, and turned around and walked out through the still open door before the governor's secretary closed it behind her.

"So why'd you bring her here anyway?" the governor asked. "She's undocumented."

"That's why I brought her here, Governor. She helped me out of Juárez in exchange for passage into the United States. Now I'm going to make sure she gets that documentation."

"You know her brother's involved in all this CLA stuff?"

"Yes Governor. She told me as much, and I was there during her debriefing."

"I don't think you understand Ned," said Senator Andreaz. "The CLA wasn't on anyone's radar until after you got back from Juárez, but now that we've looked into their CIA file, we know a lot more. It turns out that Miss Madero's brother is one of the leaders in their organization."

"Yeah," said the governor. "He's not the top dog, but he's pretty high on the food chain."

"So the CIA does have agents on the inside," said Ned.

"Not exactly," replied the senator. "The agents in Juárez were working with informants on the inside, but everything's gone dark since last night. We think the Chihuahuans might have hit the CIA office in Juárez."

"I heard there was something going on in New Mexico too," said Ned. "Do we know what that's about?"

"That," said Senator Andreaz. "Is why we've started grounding planes. Who knows how far these terrorist attacks are going to go."

"What attacks, Senator? What's happened in New Mexico?"

"The CLA blew up the Elephant Butte Dam," said the governor.

"They blew up the Elephant Butte Dam?" asked Ned.

"That's what I said," replied the governor. "The bastards blew up the stinking dam."

"It looks like that was their plan from the beginning." Senator Andreaz looked at Ned. "Control the Dams in El Paso, then destroy the Elephant Butte Dam. The water released from the reservoir will flood their dried out farms with irrigation water. It's subtle politics for sure, but the issue of water rights is one that a lot of people will get behind, especially during a drought."

"You think they're playing politics?" asked Ned.

"You can't build an army without playing some politics," said the governor. "Before there was General Washington, there was the Continental Congress."

"But, aren't there other dams along the way to El Paso?" asked Ned. "And won't the water flood every town along the way?"

"The city of Truth or Consequences, New Mexico sits below the dam, and has already been destroyed. There are dozens dead, hundreds missing. With all the water, the Rio Grande is completely flooding all its banks and even cutting new paths along the way, and every town in its path is in danger. We've already ordered some evacuations, and the president will be addressing congress soon. There's one more major reservoir downstream, but it's expected to fail once the water from the Elephant Butte gets there."

"How long until that happens?"

Senator Andreaz looked at his watch. "Probably less than hour. After that, the water will pick up speed again for a while. There are other dams downstream, but they're only irrigation dams, and the water is expected to run over them. We're not sure if it can be contained through Las Cruces so that entire city may need to be evacuated, even though it's not expected to be terribly destructive at that point; probably survivable."

"When will it get to El Paso?" asked Ned

"The water won't get to El Paso until later this evening. Maybe around nine o'clock. When it does, it will have lost most of its destructive energy, but we still expect it to put all of the low lying areas of El Paso and Juárez, including both downtowns, under several feet of water."

"So what are we going to do?" asked Ned.

"What this means," the governor responded. "Is that whatever we're going to do, if we don't do it by tonight, we'll have to wait until the water's cleared. It'll start going down almost as soon as it gets there, but it'll leave a ton of damage and debris as it passes through. Even then, it's the time of year that snow melt is usually filling up that reservoir, so it could be that the river will be raging for some time. And pray it doesn't rain."

"But what can we do by this evening?"

"Well," the governor continued. "The president has ordered all National Guard and Reserve Units to be ready for call up. Most of them can't get to El Paso today of course, but he's also ordered every spare active duty and reserve soldier in Texas and other nearby states to get to Fort Bliss asap. The thought is that by six o'clock this evening, there'll be at least enough soldiers to take back the city, if the president has the stomach for it."

"He'll take back El Paso," said the senator. "The real question is if there will be any further response. Even though we've been trying to keep this story under wraps, people have already been crying for blood. There are those that think the Mexican government must have been complicit in the attack and want a military retaliation. They just don't believe that this insurgent army could be so well organized without help from the Mexican government."

"But Mexico City would never be involved in something like this," said Ned.

"Of course not," said the governor. "They've got less spine than the fools in Washington." He looked at the senator, then back to Ned. "Present company excepted of course."

"Of course," said the senator.

"You said that the president will be addressing congress," said Ned. "Do we know what he's going to say?"

"Not exactly," answered the senator. "But we do know he'll be asking for congressional approval for whatever military response he has planned. He has the authority to defend the country from attack, which is why I'm certain he will retake El Paso, but he's on shaky legal ground if he decides to take the military across the border into Mexico without congressional approval."

"He doesn't need approval for a legitimate counterstrike," the governor interjected.

"There's also the question of how the international community will respond to any retaliation against Mexico. There's a certain school of thought that any use of force resolution won't be enough to make the important international players happy. We're Mexico's biggest trading partner, but there are still other nations that will work on behalf of Mexico's interests."

"That's all a bunch of hooey nonsense," said the governor. "We're talking about the invasion of a major American city here. There hasn't been anything like this since the bombing of Pearl Harbor, and you have to go all the way back to the 1800s to find a bona fide invasion force."

"Regardless," said the senator. "We won't know exactly what the president will say to congress until it happens. We won't have to wait long though. He's making his address at two o'clock."

Ned checked his watch. It was a quarter after one.

Just then, the phone on the governor's desk rang.

"Yes," the governor said into the phone. "What? A video? Okay, come on in, and bring that girl with you."

"Jeanine says there's some kind of video we need to see. She's got it queued up to play on the monitor here."

There was a television monitor hanging on the wall opposite the governor's desk. The secretary came into the room and Lisa followed behind her.

"This video was uploaded an hour ago," said the governor's secretary. "But it's already been watched thousands of times. I just got a notice from the president's staff that you should watch it immediately."

The three men stood around the television as the video started.

Jack Stuart was on the screen. Ned recognized the setting as the courtroom from his farce of a trial by the Chihuahuan Liberation Army.

There was a man on the witness stand that Ned didn't recognize.

"Ned Albrecht," said Jack to the man on the witness stand. "You stand accused, on behalf of your government, the United States of America, of stealing Chihuahuan land, terrorizing the Chihuahuan people, and illegally regulating the flow of water into the city of Ciudad Juárez. How do you plead?"

Chapter Twenty-Nine

The trial in the video went on more or less in the same fashion as the one that Ned had taken part in. It looked like they found someone else to play the part of Ned and reshot the entire proceedings. It certainly wasn't word for word the same as the first trial, but the broad strokes were all there, and it was probably even more effective to have the defendant in on the production. After the video, a man who identified himself as the supreme leader of the CLA took credit for both the invasion of El Paso and the destruction of the Elephant Butte Dam.

The video was only about twenty minutes long, even though Ned's trial had lasted nearly an hour. So they either didn't shoot nearly as much footage, thought Ned, or they did a crackerjack job of editing the video for time.

"I guess it didn't do very much good to retrieve the video files after all," said Ned, looking over at Lisa.

"At least it's not your face on the witness stand," said the senator. "It will be a lot easier to discredit this way."

The governor's secretary turned the television to a network news feed of the Capitol Building in Washington D.C. It was nearly time for the president to address congress, and it didn't look like it was going to be delayed.

"Mister Speaker," a congressman shouted. "The President of the United States."

There was clapping and cheering that lasted for several minutes as the president made his way to the podium.

"Congressmen. Senators. My fellow Americans. At approximately five o'clock this morning, Mountain Time, the border between the Mexican City of Juárez and the American city of El Paso was overrun by a Mexican insurgent group that calls itself the Chihuahuan Liberation Army. This group then proceeded to invade El Paso, and now occupies much of the city. This same group is also responsible for the destruction of the Elephant Butte Dam in New Mexico, and the still growing number of American dead related to both of these events."

"In 1941, the last time an American City was attacked by a governmental foreign power, President Roosevelt called it a day that will live in infamy, because of the unprovoked and dastardly nature of the attack by the lawful government of a foreign power. Today's attack varies from that one in that the official government of Mexico did not approve of, or aid in this invasion. Therefore, we cannot hold the government of

Mexico responsible for this reprehensible attack."

"We can, however, hold the government of Mexico liable for failing to control its citizenry in relation to our border in El Paso. It is our responsibility to keep our border secure, but it is also Mexico's responsibility to control its own population so that it cannot engage in acts or war upon its neighbors. And make no mistake. This is an act of war. This is an invasion of the United States by a foreign army, and we must respond in kind if we are to maintain the justice and domestic tranquility that is outlined in the preamble of our constitution."

"Under the authority granted to me by the United States Constitution as Supreme Commander of the Armed Forces, I will be retaking the city of El Paso and pressing into Juárez to eliminate the threat of this so-called liberation army. We cannot abide the threat of invasion along our southern border, and we will make it secure once more."

"I will once again reiterate. It was Mexico's responsibility to ensure that its citizens did not wage war upon the United States of America. For their government to have failed so spectacularly in this manner, is for Mexico to have failed as a state. I ask that congress declare war on the United Mexican States until such time as Mexico is once again able to properly govern its citizenry."

"Congressmen. Senators. My fellow Americans. May God bless the people of El Paso today, and may God bless the United States of America."

Chapter Thirty

"Well that was dramatic," said Governor Foster.

"Governor."

"Yes Jeanine."

"The president's office would like to set up a teleconference with Mister Albrecht."

"Set it up. We'll take it here."

"Actually sir, the president would like a private meeting with Mister Albrecht and Miss Madero."

"Oh, uh, okay." The governor looked around the room. "They can still use my office. I'm past due for a lunch break anyway. Join me Senator?"

"I take it we're not going too far?"

"Just the cafeteria dining room downstairs."

"Sounds delightful." The senator then looked at Ned. "I'll

talk to you later." The senator then followed the governor out of the office and toward the elevator.

***

Ned and Lisa had continued to watch the coverage of the president's speech. He slowly made it out of the congressional hall shaking many hands along the way. It was about ten minutes later that the teleconference call came through.

"Mister Albrecht," The president said. "I'm sorry I never got a chance to meet you in Washington. We haven't met, have we Ned? Can I call you Ned, by the way?"

"Absolutely Mister President, and I believe we shook hands at one of the senator's fundraisers, but that was about it."

"Oh yeah, that time in Dallas, of course, and you're Miss Madero. I've got to tell you something. I really hope the two of you can help me out here."

"Anything we can do, Mister President"

"Good, Good. You know, I've got half my staff telling me I'm off my rocker calling you two right now. I've got a dozen world leaders waiting to talk to me. Let 'em wait, that's what I say. They just want to tell me I'm being a bully to Mexico. What about you Miss Madero, do you think I'm being a bully to Mexico?"

"Well, they did attack first."

"See," said the president. "Even the Mexican girl understands."

"But that's not to say they weren't provoked by a lot of your government's policies." Lisa added quickly.

"Yes, I know," said the president. "No one could have foreseen how hard the deportation program was going to hit the Mexican economy, and this drought isn't making life any easier for anybody, but that's all water under the bridge now, no pun intended. What we need to do now is address the current crisis, and stabilize the whole situation. That's where I need your help, the both of you. This Chihuahuan Liberation Army of yours is practically hanging themselves, what with their claiming of responsibility for the destruction of these dams. It's not enough for them to attack El Paso, but they've got to go and destroy our infrastructure too. Still, it would be helpful if we could capture one of their leaders; someone who we could use to put their organization on trial."

"Like they put Ned on trial in Mexico." Lisa stared coldly at the president.

"Kind of," said the president. "Same ends, but we'll use different means. It will be a fair trial, and we won't make any one individual answer for the crimes of the CLA. We'll put the individuals on trial, if necessary, and we'll use the individuals as witnesses in a trial against the CLA, if it's politically expedient that is."

"So you want to capture someone," said Ned. "But who is it exactly, Mister President, that you want to capture, and how can we help?"

"Well, there's the thing Ned. We would love to have their supreme leader, and of course Jack Stuart would be a great catch, but if we could turn one of their leader's to our side, that would be even better. And since Miss Madero's brother is in a prime position, we would like the two of you to head back into Juárez, ahead of the counter-invasion force, and see if you can't convince him to come along quietly."

"You want us to go back into Juárez now, alone?" Lisa didn't look like she was warming to the president at all.

"Well, we could send a military group with you, or a CIA handler, that's up to you two, but I thought you might just want to travel light and lean. I read the reports about how you escaped back into El Paso. The two of you worked well together, and that might be the best way to go back in."

"No," said Lisa. "I'm not going back."

"Don't make up your mind too soon now."

"Mister President," Ned interrupted. "I will serve at your pleasure, but you can't expect the same from Miss Madero. She risked her life helping me get out of Juárez so that she could escape what that city has become."

"I know that Ned, and I'm not going to force her to go. I won't even make any veiled threats about imprisonment or deportation. She's here, she helped us out, and she can stay."

"What I'm offering you, Miss Madero," the president continued. "Is a presidential order that declares you a citizen of the United States and gives you a government pension. The pension isn't extravagant, but it's enough so that you could pursue what you want to do without having to worry about your basic expenses."

"So what do you want, Miss Madero? You could struggle with years of paperwork to maintain a resident visa, or you could go through the tedious process of naturalization, or you could have it all right now. I have the order here in front of me. One stroke of my pen, and you're a citizen of the world. All you have to do, is say yes."

Chapter Thirty-One

Lisa told Ned that the decision wasn't difficult. So many times she had cursed the fact that a simple piece of paper was all that kept her from returning to El Paso after the immigration reform act had become law. Now she had a signed presidential order that declared her a citizen of the United States.

After speaking with the president, and before heading back to El Paso, Ned and Lisa had a brief conversation with Senator Andreaz. The senator told them that congress had wasted no time in passing a declaration of war against Mexico. The declaration authorized the president to, take any and all actions necessary to regain American lands and to stabilize the border and the government of Mexico, until such time as peace was established either by treaty with

Mexico or by resolution of congress. The declaration had not been unanimous, but won by overwhelming margins in both chambers. Most of the dissent was from the Northeastern and Northwestern states, but even the representatives from those areas fell mostly in line.

The senator also told Ned that he didn't have to go back to El Paso if he didn't want to, and that he really didn't appreciate the president stealing his chief aide out from under him. After they said their goodbyes, Ned and Lisa found themselves back on the same military plane that had flown them into Austin just a few hours earlier. The only difference was that the plane was now nearly full of United States Army reservists.

"So what exactly is the plan here?" Lisa asked Ned.

"That depends," said Ned. "Will we be able to convince your brother to turn against the CLA?"

"I don't know. He always seemed pretty loyal to them. At least, as much as he's ever been loyal to anything. I used to think he would be loyal to me, but when the army gave him more responsibility, he didn't seem to care anything about what I had to say. Still, we've been given quite a lot to offer him. He'll get a better deal than I did, if he'll take it." Lisa paused a moment. "Never underestimate the power of greed."

"That certainly isn't a ringing endorsement of human integrity," said Ned.

"It wasn't supposed to be."

"If you think he can be reasoned with, the best course of action will be to find him and convince him to come with us.

Do you know how we can find him?"

"There are several possibilities. The headquarters that we escaped from is one. He could also be out with one of the fighting groups, in which case, it will be a lot more difficult. I think what we should do is start at my restaurant. He probably won't be there, but the security won't be as high as if we go to the headquarters, and I might find someone there who I can trust, who will tell me where he is."

"That sounds like a good plan. Where exactly is the restaurant?"

"It's east of the headquarters. Not even a kilometer. Near the Viaducto Diaz Ordaz."

"All right then," said Ned. "That's where we'll start. I don't know where our point of entry will be yet. We'll have to wait for the general's briefing before we make further plans. Maybe we should try and get some more sleep. It might be a long night tonight."

"I'm not really tired." She paused a moment. "Ned, what do you think about all this?"

"What do you mean?" asked Ned. "All of this?"

"I mean, the war, the deportations, the relationship between our two countries."

"Our two countries," said Ned. "Don't forget, the United States is your country now too."

"Yes, I know, but I'll always be from Mexico, even if I never go back after today."

"I know what you mean," said Ned. "So you want my thoughts on the relationship between the United States and

Mexico. I guess it's a good thing we have some time here, because that could take a while to explain."

"You know that I work for a senator that was at the forefront of the immigration reform act. So you must realize some of my political leanings."

"Yes," said Lisa. "But I also know that political opinions can be complicated, and from the time I broke you out of that prison, you never seemed like someone who hates Mexicans."

"You think that everyone who wants to control immigration hates immigrants?"

"No," said Lisa. "Of course not, but it seems like the people who wanted that law passed wanted to punish Mexicans, and it really has only seemed to hurt Mexico."

"There were consequences here as well," said Ned. "Almost everything that was related to cheap labor shot up in price. The cost of domestic produce almost doubled, and the small-farm organic farmers made out like bandits, since they were about the only ones who didn't need to raise their prices. Construction, household, and service industries suffered too."

"I know, for you, things cost more. For us in Juárez, we were destitute, and sometimes starving."

"You're right. Mexico was definitely hit harder than the United States. When most of your trade is with one country, and that one country stops trading, it's going to hurt. And I'm sorry."

"So you didn't approve of the trade embargo?"

"No," said Ned. "I never thought that was a good idea,

but there were those who thought that any transit across the border in El Paso, even that of goods, would make a path for illegal entry."

"So you did approve of stopping the illegal entry?"

"Yes, I've always felt that any immigration, or migrant workers program, should be approved by congress, and therefore, lawful in its nature. It just always rubbed me the wrong way that people were entering the country illegally. We are, after all, a nation of laws. But it isn't as simple as just saying that. My own mother often tells me that Mexicans are hard workers, and she doesn't see why they shouldn't come here if they want to work."

"And what do you tell her?"

"That it isn't as simple as that. When we fail to control the border, we don't only get the honest hard-working Mexicans. We also get people who would certainly be turned away if they were to try and come into the country legally. I've always felt that one of the major problems is that we don't allow enough migrant workers into the country. If we had a migrant workers program that brought in millions of Mexican workers that could stay in the country for up to a year and then return home for several months before coming back, that would solve a lot of problems on both sides of the border."

"Yes," said Lisa. "I've heard your senator talk about this plan. Do you think it will happen?"

"A couple of days ago," said Ned. "I would have said yes. I think we were on track to pass the legislation in the next few months, and we would have started bringing in migrants early next year. We could've even started diverting people who were scheduled for deportation. But, I think this business in El Paso has changed everything."

"Changed everything." Lisa thought about this for a moment. "So, how do you think we got here? I mean, what went so wrong that the United States felt it had to start deporting people by the hundreds of thousands."

"I'd say it's been building for a long time, and a lot of it doesn't even have so much to do with the immigrants. I think a lot of the conflict has more to do with the people in this country not agreeing on what to do about the problem. Some people not even acknowledging that there was a problem."

"You had some people, who wanted to make certain that there was no illegal entry, and wanted to deport everyone who had come into the country illegally. Then there were other people, who thought that our country had a duty to take care of anyone who could make it to our soil, and they didn't want to send anyone back under any circumstances. That was actually the most popular notion in some parts of the country, and you even had some cities that set themselves up as so-called sanctuary cities."

"I know all about the sanctuary cities," said Lisa. For all the good they did in the end."

"It is true that once the administration decided to start enforcing federal law, there wasn't much that local statute could do to get in the way."

"Anyway, there were also a lot of people on both sides

who weren't so caught up in the issue but, like me, didn't like the idea of people flouting the law so deliberately. It wasn't even so much the illegal entry, as it was the other Americans who didn't seem to want to enforce the law."

"I think that the people who were so opposed to any kind of immigration reform eventually provoked a backlash from those who wanted the law enforced, and immigration reform ended up becoming the most important issue in national politics."

"I guess that makes sense," said Lisa. But it sounds like quite a lot of guesswork."

"I suppose it does at that. In the end, the two sides just wouldn't work together on any kind of reform. Then, after it blew up into such a big issue, the pro-reform politicians were elected, and this is what we're left with. I certainly think it would have been better to integrate something like the senator's migrant worker program into the reform act. It could have avoided a lot of the deportations if people had signed up to be migrant workers and voluntarily returned to Mexico with the understanding that they would be able to come back every year. But people were impatient for change, so the reform act was passed, the border crossings were shut down, and the deportations began."

"Do you think there was anything that could have avoided this?" asked Lisa.

"Other than the two sides working together sooner, I don't think it could have been avoided. But then, the two sides were never going to work together."

"You had one side that thought the other side didn't care at all about the law or defending the nation's borders. Then you had the other side that thought the first side was clearly xenophobic and completely overreacting to a problem that didn't really seem to matter. Both sides started at unreasonable positions, and you can't have a reasonable argument with someone starting out with an unreasonable position."

"So you think we were doomed from the beginning?"

"Not doomed, but it does seem like it was almost inevitable. The underlying problem has always been the economic insecurity that people face in Mexico. Anytime there has ever been a way to pick up and move to try and make your life better, some people will pick up and move. Nothing short of stabilizing the Mexican economy to the point that it was on par with that of the United States would have kept people from trying to come across the border in such numbers."

"You know, I used to tell people that the United States should have just kept all of Mexico at the end of the Mexican—American War. Then we wouldn't have hardly any of the problems we have today. You know, one government, one economy."

"You don't still think that would have been a good idea?"

"Well, not realistic anyway. I once had a conversation with a history professor about my idea. She said that it never could have happened because the United States wouldn't have wanted so many brown, Catholic, Spanish speaking people as citizens."

"Do you think that's true?"

"I think there's some truth to it, but it really got me thinking. So I looked into other reasons why the United States might not have wanted all of Mexico, and came to the decision that it was mostly about slavery."

"Slavery?"

"Yeah. Keep in mind that the Mexican—American War was only about fifteen years before the American Civil War, and that slavery had already been completely abolished in Mexico. Mexico had about twenty states back then, but allowing Mexico to come into the United States as even ten new states would have greatly upset the balance of power. If the Mexican states had sided with the free northern states, the slave states would have been completely outnumbered in both houses, and it's unlikely that any candidate from a slaveholding state could have ever been elected president."

"So slavery is the reason that Mexico isn't part of the United States?" Lisa sounded skeptical.

"Well," said Ned. "That's my opinion anyway. What do you think?"

"I don't know that much about American history, and that's not how they taught the Mexican—American War where I went to school, but I don't think it could have just been about slavery." She paused for a moment, and then looked at Ned. "I think maybe your history professor was right. The Americans didn't want the Mexicans to be part of the United States, just like they don't today."

Chapter Thirty-Two

After landing at the airfield, Ned and Lisa were met once again by Private Philips and his transport vehicle.

"You know Philips," said Ned, once they were on their way. "If you weren't otherwise engaged, I think I'd have to hire you out as my personal driver."

"Does that mean I should ask you for a job once my enlistment is over?"

"Let's take this one day at a time private. Where are we off to now?"

"To see another familiar face," the private replied. "Captain Smith will be briefing you on your mission."

"I see. No meeting with the general, then?"

"No sir, the general is coordinating the counteroffensive, which has already sort-of begun."

"What do you mean?" asked Ned. "I was told we were going in ahead of the assault."

"Yes sir, I believe you're going in ahead of the main assault, but we've already been working to take back the green zone. It hasn't really been that difficult. Our troops have been flooding in all day from across Texas, and the CLA never really moved very far across the border. They're mostly spread out along the river, except where they're holding the dams and the deportation port. The port is where we'll be establishing a beachhead into Juárez to help facilitate the counterassault."

They drove south through the green zone on Airport Road, and then on East Paisano Drive. It really didn't seem that different from the drive Ned had taken to see Director Rodriguez the day before. There were no signs of conflict in the streets, but there were a lot of military vehicles on the road. Private Philips told them that they were heading to the grounds of the El Paso Zoo, where the counterassault into Juárez was being staged.

As they got closer to the zoo, Ned could hear the sounds of battle. When the vehicle stopped, Captain Smith was waiting, dressed in his class A dress uniform.

"What's the occasion, Captain?" asked Ned.

"I'll be going with you into Juárez," the captain replied. "I have a side mission that shouldn't delay you too much. And don't ask me what it is. You'll know soon enough."

"It sounds like the fighting's still going on," said Ned.

"They've already established a perimeter for the outpost

in Juárez, but the damn CLA fighters keep trying to take it back. Satellite imagery shows that they don't have the forces for an all-out assault unless they abandon at least one of the dam sites, but they keep sending in squads to get mowed down."

They all went into a tent that had a map of both El Paso and Juárez on a table.

Captain Smith motioned to the map. "Now show me exactly where you want to start your search for Miss Madero's brother."

Lisa looked at the map and then put her finger on an intersection near the Viaducto Diaz Ordaz. "Right here is where our restaurant is."

"All right," said the captain. "That will work just fine. We will be detouring here." He pointed at an avenue further south called the Ejército Nacional.

"The National Army Highway," said Ned. "Is that some kind of joke?"

The captain glowered at Ned. "I didn't name the road, Mister Albrecht. We just need to get there."

"But it's practically in the opposite direction of where we need to go."

"Don't worry, Mister Albrecht. It won't take too long. We'll have transportation."

The captain then walked them outside and showed them an old beat-up purple Volkswagen Jetta with Mexican license plates.

Chapter Thirty-Three

There was another squad of CLA soldiers assaulting the beachhead while they were making their exit into Juárez. Ned thought he heard some bullets fly by the car as the CLA soldiers were taking potshots at them. Fortunately, none of them hit.

It wasn't long before they were all driving south. Captain Smith was driving, Private Philips was in the front passenger seat, and Ned and Lisa were in the back. The car would have blended in perfectly in Juárez, except for the fact that there was hardly any traffic on the streets. The people must have been staying at home, or had already moved into El Paso, because it was like a ghost town.

It took about twenty minutes to travel the four miles to the National Army Highway. Once there, they headed east.

"Get those binoculars out private," ordered the captain. "And tell me if you see anything up ahead."

"I take it this is part of your secret mission, Captain?" asked Ned.

"Umm, Captain." Private Philips sounded like he didn't want to interrupt. "I see something."

"Well, what is it private?"

"Umm, it… It looks like an army sir."

Chapter Thirty-Four

Before long, Ned could begin to make out the army up ahead without the aid of binoculars. They were moving very slowly. It looked like they had several military-style combat vehicles, including five-ton trucks, and the same kind of vehicle that Private Philips had been using to ferry Ned around in El Paso. In addition to the vehicles, it looked like there were multiple columns of soldiers marching in line as far as the eye could see.

They continued to drive slowly east until a shot was fired in their direction. Then a voice from a bullhorn said, "This is the El Paso Valley Militia. That was a warning shot. Get off the road, or we'll consider you enemy combatants."

Captain Smith then picked up the corded microphone that was part of the vehicle's radio communication system, flipped a switch on the dashboard that activated the public address system and said, "This is Captain Robert Smith of the United States Army. I have been sent to establish communication between your forces and the commanding general in El Paso, in order that we might coordinate our strikes."

There was a brief pause before the voice spoke again. "Get out of the car and proceed on foot. Bring your credentials. Leave your weapons in the car."

"Okay Ned," said the captain. "Philips and I are going to go and have a chat with these boys. You two come up to the front seat. If this goes sideways, I want you to take the car and proceed with your mission. If all goes well, however, I'll be back in a few minutes, and we can decide how to proceed together."

***

It didn't go sideways. Private Philips came back to the car after about five minutes, hopped into the backseat, and told them to drive ahead. Once they reached the army, Philips brought Ned and Lisa into the back of a truck that was the makeshift militia headquarters. Captain Smith and another man were looking over a map of Juárez. It might have been the same map the captain had showed them back in El Paso.

"Ned. You're here. Good." The captain turned away from the table. "This is General Hirsch of the El Paso Valley Militia. Our satellite scans picked up their movement earlier this afternoon, but we didn't realize they were heading into Juárez until it was too late to establish contact."

Ned knew about the independent militias throughout Texas, although he wasn't specifically familiar with any in the El Paso area. They were generally volunteer groups that trained in order to aid the government in times of need, or overthrow the government in times of tyranny. The men here were dressed mostly like ranch workers, but the general was wearing a uniform of sorts.

"This, General Hirsch, is Mister Ned Albrecht," said the captain. "He's on a secret mission for the president."

"Really?" General Hirsch seemed very intrigued. "Is it something to do with us? How can we help?"

"It doesn't really have anything to do with your forces exactly, General, but we would appreciate it if you could give him some space to do his work. It's important, and it'll be a lot more difficult once the main assault begins."

The captain then looked to Ned. "Do you have any questions for the general?"

"How big is your force General, and what exactly are you doing in Juárez?"

"We've got twenty-four hundred men, in four battalions of six hundred men each. We mustered this morning, after the attack on Juárez, and headed out after the president declared war on Mexico. We thought we should do our part. We made our way from Fabens, that's where we're headquartered, took the old border station at Socorro from the CLA forces there, and have been making our way downtown. Figured we'd run into the main CLA forces from behind, but we haven't found too many yet. Now that you all are here, I expect we'll have better intelligence."

"That's right General," said Captain Smith. "Ned has detailed information about the CLA headquarters, as does Miss Madero here. But first we need to figure out a few things. Exactly how long, General, will it take you to move your army here?" The captain put his finger on the map at the location of the CLA headquarters.

"I expect if we start marching now, we could be there in less than an hour."

"That's good," said Captain Smith. "Our tentative schedule calls for an assault at around seven p.m. If your forces can assault the headquarters at the same time that the Army forces in El Paso assault the dams and secure the border, we will be in business."

"Ned, that means you'll have a little over an hour to conduct your business. Will that be enough time?"

"There's no way to be certain, Captain. But I'll tell you what. It'll have to be."

"Good man," said the captain, and beamed approvingly. "Philips and I will be staying here with the militia. Will you and Miss Madero be okay on your own?"

"I'm sure we'll make do Captain. We were planning on just the two of us anyway." Ned paused for a moment. "It would help if we got to keep the car."

"Of course you can have the car. Now if there isn't anything else, we should start the briefing for the general, and then you two can be on you way."

"Captain," said General Hirsch. "I know that they're on

a secret mission, but if I might offer a man to go with them. Kevin! Get on up here." A young man dressed like a cowboy and wearing a six-shooter stepped forward. "This is my boy Kevin. He's good in a fight, knows his weapons, and went to the police academy in San Antonio before he decided to go to lawyer school out east. He'd be a fine addition to the team."

Captain Smith smiled. "Why, I think that's a fine idea."

Chapter Thirty-Five

Captain Smith gave General Hirsch a short briefing on the Chihuahuan Liberation Army's Headquarters, with both Ned and Lisa supplying a few details about the different buildings. Lisa was especially knowledgeable about the internal layout and function of the warehouse complex.

Most surprisingly was that, unless something had been added, there were no fortifications around the complex. All planning had gone into assaulting the border and the dam locations in El Paso, and not into defending their own city or base of operations. Their success at hiding the headquarters from the United States Military somewhat explained the lack of fortification, but it's as if they never even contemplated the idea of an attack against them. With this lack of defense, even the militia's limited forces should be able to take control of the headquarters without too much trouble, assuming that most of the CLA forces were otherwise occupied.

After the meeting, on their way back to the car, Ned took Captain Smith aside for a private conversation.

"I don't know why you accepted the general's son to be part of our mission so quickly. We don't really know anything about him and I don't know how he can be an asset."

"You're in politics, son," the captain replied. "I shouldn't have to tell you what a good will gesture can do. Look, we want General Hirsch to accept our help, and by accept our help, I mean follow our orders. If we accept his help in the form of taking his kid along for your mission, he's more likely to accept ours."

"Now that, I understand." Ned looked again at Captain Smith. "You're not like any soldier I ever met before."

"Well I wear a lot of hats. Today I'm an Army field captain, but I've worked for Army Intelligence, the NSA, and the CIA. It's a valuable skill to be adaptable."

"Now I'm sure that the boy will be fine." The captain looked over at Kevin, and then he walked over to the trunk of the car and opened it. "There's an extra sat phone and weapons here. Are you going to need anything else for your mission?"

Ned surveyed the contents of the trunk. There were two assault rifles, two handguns, a box of grenades, walkie-talkies, an emergency radio, and the satellite phone. Ned was already carrying a handgun and a sat phone.

"I'm sure I can make do with all of this."

"All right then Ned, we'll be assaulting the compound around seven if I haven't heard from you before then. But I've got to tell you. It's going to be a coordinated attack. The US Army will be taking the two dam sites and key border stations at the same time as our assault. So there'll be no way to delay this thing, once it gets rolling."

The captain raised his hand in a salute. "Safe travels Ned."

"And you, Captain."

Chapter Thirty-Six

It was a twenty minute drive to the Madero restaurant. This time around, Ned was driving the car, Lisa was in the front passenger seat, and Kevin Hirsch was riding in the back. Once they were on their way, Ned gave Kevin an abridged description of their mission and where they were heading.

"So Kevin," said Ned. "Your father said you're going to law school."

"Yup, three semesters in last fall before my dad called me back to help him manage the pecan ranch. It was getting harder to find good help with all the trouble in El Paso."

"Are you going back next fall then?" asked Ned.

"That is the plan. I'm on a leave of absence now, but I can't keep that up for more than two semesters without extenuating circumstances."

"Where do you go to school?" asked Lisa.

"Massachusetts."

"Harvard?" asked Ned.

"No, not Harvard. Boston College Law."

"Why Massachusetts?" asked Lisa.

"Well, I did apply to Harvard, and while I was applying there, I looked into the area, and decided to apply to a couple other Boston area law schools. Boston College was the first to accept my application, and that's where I decided to go."

"Your father also mentioned an interest in Law enforcement," said Ned.

"Yes, that's what my undergraduate degree was in. Criminal Justice. I always had romantic notions about being a police officer. I even dreamed of being a Texas Ranger when I was a kid. But I was always more interested in the law classes, and after a week on the job in San Antonio, I decided that I wanted to change gears and go to law school. My dad wanted me to go to a Texas school, again, but I wanted to broaden my horizons, so I looked out east."

"Tired of life in the West Texas desert?" asked Ned.

"No, it wasn't that. I just didn't want to settle down without feeling that I'd seen a little bit more of the world. And not just for a vacation, but feeling like I'd lived in it. I mean, I spent more than four years in San Antonio, but it didn't really feel that different. Then, maybe after I'd lived somewhere other than Texas, then I could come back home."

"Well Massachusetts is definitely different from Texas. New England is like its own little corner of the country. It doesn't really feel quite like anywhere else. It might even be safe to say it's more alien from Texas than northern Mexico."

"I don't know if I can agree with you there," said Kevin. "But the weather was definitely alien. Sometimes it snows in Texas, but when it started to snow in Boston in December, I'd never seen anything like that. It just sat there for days, piling up on the sidewalks and boulevards as the plows went by, and then more snow piling on top of that."

"Yes, the snow," said Ned. "I've spent many Christmases in Pennsylvania. There's really nothing like the mountains of snow. Everyone in my family complains about it, but I think most of them would be lost without it."

As they approached the restaurant, there was more activity on the streets. Lisa guided Ned until they were about a block away and parked the car.

"You mind staying with the car?" asked Ned, as he handed Kevin a walkie-talkie. "This should just be reconnaissance, but I'll radio if I need anything."

"Sure thing boss. I'll keep the getaway car ready."

Chapter Thirty-Seven

Lisa brought Ned into the restaurant through a back entrance that came into a room with some lockers, a table, and a bathroom off to the side. It was mostly quiet outside of the building and in the back, but Ned could hear men carousing in the dining area. They crept quietly into the kitchen where there was one man making burritos. The man was big and tall, and looked like he was in his fifties, with graying hair underneath his chef's hat.

"Jorge," said Lisa quietly, but loud enough for the man working over the stove to hear.

"Felisa?" The man looked up and then ran over and wrapped her in a big bear hug.

"They told me you were gone," the man said in Spanish. "They said you helped the gringo escape." The man then looked at Ned and his eyes became wide. "You did help the gringo escape. Mija, what are you doing back here. They'll kill you if they find you."

"I need to find Alonzo. Do you know where he is?"

"Oh Felisa, he was here. I tried to ask him about you, and he looked worried, but he wouldn't say anything. Then he was called away."

"Do you know where he went?"

"The army moved most of their soldiers to the international dam site. You know, the one just up the road. I'm certain that's where your brother went."

"Thank you Jorge. I've got to follow him now."

"But mija, why do you need to find him now?"

"There's something coming Jorge. Do you understand? And I've got to get him out now, for his own good."

"I understand Felisa. Do you want me to come too? I can help you."

"No Jorge, I have enough help, and you need to help your family. You need to keep them safe now."

"I understand. You go now. I'll stay here and take care of my family." The man gave her another hug. "Goodbye mija."

Ned and Lisa then crept out of the kitchen and into the back room. Lisa opened one of the lockers, grabbed a pile of uniforms, and put them in a bag that was hanging on a hook. Less than a minute later, they were back in the car, which was ready to go, just as Kevin had promised.

"Will your friend tell anyone he saw us?" asked Ned.

"He's worked at our restaurant since before my brother

was born. He was almost like a second father to us. He would never betray me, not even to my brother. Plus, he's never liked the CLA anyway."

"How far is the dam?" asked Ned.

"About three kilometers," said Lisa. "It won't take long to get there."

"If we had more time, I might call for satellite reconnaissance, but I'm afraid we're just going to have to wing it."

"You may have time. We need to change into these uniforms if we're going to walk into that camp, and my house is just a couple blocks north of here."

"They won't be looking for you there?" asked Ned.

"I don't think so. Last night, they would have, but not now. And with my brother gone, it should be safe."

Lisa pointed Ned toward the house in question, and he parked the car around the corner in front a two matching palm trees. Ned, Lisa, and Kevin all got out of the car and walked to the house. Lisa unlocked the door with a security code, and they all went inside.

Lisa dumped the bag that she had filled at the restaurant. "We keep extra uniforms at the restaurant for the soldiers. Find one that fits and put it on. My brother might have some in that room too." She pointed at one of the doors, and then went into one of the other bedrooms.

"I would have expected your family to have a bigger house than this," Ned shouted through the door as he and Kevin changed.

"We do," Lisa shouted back. "It's south of town. We kept this house so that if we worked late at the restaurant, we'd have somewhere nearby to sleep for the night."

"Must be rough," Kevin said quietly to Ned, who looked back at Kevin.

"Don't judge her too harshly, she's lost everything now that she once had, and I bet your ranch house is bigger than this one too."

"Yeah, you're right there."

"Not to mention the cost of Boston College Law School."

"All right, I see your point."

Lisa came back out of the room dressed in the same fashion as she had been the first time Ned saw her. Ned and Kevin were also dressed in the same blue uniform style of the Chihuahuan Liberation Army.

Ned noticed that Lisa was wearing combat boots, with her pant legs tucked in. Ned's boots might pass, but Kevin was wearing cowboy boots. "Are we going to look out of place without the right boots?"

"No," replied Lisa." Half the soldiers wear cowboy boots." The CLA was very generous with the uniforms, but didn't provide as many boots. They want you to wear something black, but anything dark will do. Just put the pant leg over the boot."

Chapter Thirty-Eight

Ned had made his phone call for satellite reconnaissance and they were quickly on their way. The satellite recon told him that while the CLA had built massive fortifications on the El Paso side of the river, there was practically nothing on this side. It made Ned wonder if they had anyone who was familiar with military theory. If they were flanked, there would be no way for them to put up a decent defense.

Back in the car, they headed north, and before long, drove over an irrigation canal that was flowing full with water. Ned stopped the car.

"Is that the Acequia Madre?" asked Ned.

"It is," replied Lisa. "I've never seen so much water in it before. Is this where it's going to flood, do you think?"

"It's hard to say," said Ned. "It's possible that the banks of the river will overspill somewhere upstream, but we're pretty close to the Rio Grande already, and since the canal flows here, I've got to believe that this is already a pretty low lying area. Imagine another four feet of water on top of that."

Lisa's eyes went wide.

"What is this about a flood?" asked Kevin.

"You heard in the president's speech about the destruction of the Elephant Butte Dam?" said Ned.

"I did," replied Kevin.

"Well all that water's coming downstream, and there's really nothing to stop it before it gets here. It won't be moving destructively fast, but it's a lot of water, and everything in low lying areas will be flooded until it passes through."

"And when exactly is this going to happen?"

"When I talked to the satellite recon people, they said it could be as soon as eight o'clock. That's the main reason why the attack on the CLA can't be postponed. It'll be hard to move anything in this city, once that water hits."

"But how long will it last?"

"The water might start to recede in as little as an hour," said Ned. "But it will leave debris and chaos in its wake. It could delay effective military action for days or longer." Ned looked at his watch. "Speaking of time, we've got less than an hour to find Lisa's brother and get him out of there. Let's get going."

Chapter Thirty-Nine

Ned continued to drive north until they met the highway that ran parallel to the Rio Grande. As they continued to drive northwest, they could sometimes see the Acequia Madre running down the middle of the highway, like a center of the road ditch that was nearly filled to bursting with water.

As they drove along the river, they could see armed CLA forces on the far side of the river, guarding the border. It looked like they had used concrete highway barriers to build foxholes that were spaced evenly along the river's edge. The fortification line veered off as they got closer to the dam. Ned knew from his conversation with satellite recon that the fortification line circled the north side of the dam with a radius of about one kilometer, centered on the dam.

They decided to leave the car a short distance from the

dam site on a side street. The car provided a certain amount of camouflage for them, but leaving it on the road directly opposite the dam would be too conspicuous, and Ned wanted to make sure it would still be there when they got back.

They opened the trunk before leaving the car. Ned pocketed one grenade and gave another to Kevin. He then took a second pistol for himself and gave the other one to Lisa. Lastly, he handed an assault rifle to Kevin, who slung it over his shoulder.

From there, they made their way on foot the last kilometer to the dam. There were CLA soldiers coming and going, but there didn't appear to be too much organization to their effort. There had been no official border crossing here, so except for the top of the international dam, there was no bridge across the river. The riverbed below the dam, however, was currently bone dry, and that was the easiest way to get to the fortifications on the north side.

Ned, Lisa, and Kevin kept their heads down as they walked among the CLA soldiers. Once they were across the river, Lisa began to make inquiries about the location of her brother as inconspicuously as she could. Ned noticed that she referred to herself as Captain Herrerra and was telling people she was supposed to report to Colonel Madero. After finding someone who seemed to know what was going on, they were directed to a small apartment building that was being used as the command center for the dam fortifications. They arrived at the building, and watched it from a safe distance.

"It looks more like a big ranch house than an apartment

building," said Kevin. "If not for all the doors and mailboxes, that's what I'd think it was."

"Fortunately for us," said Ned. "The soldiers are coming and going here as well. We should be able to get inside without anyone noticing."

"Still," said Lisa. "It's much more likely that someone here will recognize me. And the two of you will look even more out of place. It's a real risk going inside."

"I could scout it out," said Kevin. "My mother was half Mexican, and I've been speaking Spanish since I was a baby. I should be able to blend in okay and I could ask a few questions."

Ned looked to Lisa. She shrugged.

"All right Kevin, you head inside. Try to make your way back out quickly. If you're not back here in ten minutes, we're coming in after you. If you can't get back out, you've got your walkie, and as a last resort, fire your pistol. We'll come running."

Chapter Forty

Ned and Lisa didn't have to wait the full ten minutes.

"What did you find?" asked Lisa.

"I did like you said," replied Kevin. "I found someone who didn't look too important, and I asked about who was in command. Then I asked about Colonel Madero. They said they hadn't seen him. Then I asked about Jack Stuart. They said Jack was attending to some business in the apartment next door."

Ned looked at the next building on the block. It was in the same style as the first, although not identical.

"There's no traffic going into that building," said Kevin. "We'll be noticed for sure if we walk in."

"You're right." Ned looked further up the block. There was another building that looked like some kind of business.

"Let's go," said Ned.

"Where are we going?" asked Lisa.

"I have an idea." Ned led them up the street and into the yard next door where they walked around the building and climbed over the fence before arriving at the back of the apartment building.

The sun was sinking further into the southwestern sky, but it was still daylight. If anyone was watching, they would be seen. Ned could only hope that no one was watching. The back door of the apartment building was a security door in a steel frame, and Ned knew that if it didn't open, they'd have to find another way in. Fortunately, it looked like the lock had already been broken, probably when the CLA soldiers had forced their way in. There was a stairs that went both upstairs and down, and a long hall that went straight ahead.

They entered the first door on the left side of the hall. The lock on this door was broken as well. It looked like either the CLA soldiers or looters had made their way through the entire building. The door opened into a back entryway, which then led to a small hallway that connected two bedrooms, a kitchen, a living room, and a front entryway.

This apartment was completely abandoned. It looked like the people who had left had time to pack, but still left some things behind. There was a couch in the living room, as well as an empty television mount on the wall. There was also a bed stripped bare and an empty dresser in the bedroom, as well as a table with no chairs in the kitchen.

They made their way back out of the apartment and

tried the door on the other side of the hall. It was the same layout as the first apartment in reverse. As they went down the hallway and into the kitchen, they came across three men in CLA uniforms. Two of the soldiers were seated at a table and presumably guarding the third, who was tied to a chair.

"Who are you?" asked one of the guards in Spanish.

"Hands up," ordered Kevin, and raised the rifle to point at one of the guards.

Ned pointed his handgun at the other guard. "Like he said, hands up."

Lisa was the last one to enter the room, and gasped when she saw the man tied to the chair. "That's Alonzo."

"Hey sis." Alonzo smiled. "See what you got me into here."

"You all are making a big mistake," said one of the guards, both of whom now had their hands up.

"That's right," said Kevin. "Our mistake." He pushed both of the guards' guns onto the floor, then turned the rifle around and hit one of the guards in the head with the butt of his rifle. The guard fell to the floor. Then Kevin raised the rifle again.

"Hey!" The other guard stood up.

"Not so fast," said a voice at the door.

Ned, who had been watching Kevin subdue the guards, turned to see that Jack Stuart had entered the room, and was now holding a gun to Lisa's head.

Chapter Forty-One

"Well, look at you, Mister Albrecht."

Ned's gun was now aimed directly at Jack, while Jack continued to keep his gun pointed directly at Lisa's head.

"You," Jack said to Lisa. "Get on your knees, and keep your hands up."

Lisa moved to her knees while watching Jack's gun. Then she looked directly at Ned.

"When I heard that you were back in Juárez," said Jack. "I couldn't believe it. After you escaped last night, I thought I'd never see you again. When I heard that you and the girl had returned, I couldn't think of a reason why, except that you were looking for someone she knew. That's why I brought the colonel here…"

"Still here," said Alonzo.

"Shut up!" shouted Jack. "That's why I brought the colonel here, but you were supposed to come in through the front door. Now that you've spoiled my surprise, I'm going to have to demand that you drop your guns, or I'll kill the girl."

"Come on Jack, you know I can't lower my gun now." Ned's gun was still pointed directly at Jack. "And that goes for you too." Ned glanced over at Kevin, whose rifle was pointed at the still standing guard. "If we drop our guns now, you'll just kill all three of us."

Jack smiled. "It looks like we've got a real-life Mexican standoff here. How appropriate. However, if you don't drop your guns now, I can guarantee that this girl will be the first to die."

"And you'll be the second," said Ned. "Look Jack, there's no way we're going to trust you, and you've got no hope of coming out of this anyway. The United States has declared war against Mexico. The American Army is on its way. Your plans for a free Texas have failed. When you're captured, you'll be tried for terrorism and high treason."

"Lies!" shouted Jack. "The Feds have got no stomach for war. They'll turn back once the public cries out." Jack moved his gun from Lisa to Ned. "Maybe you should be the first to die."

Ned could see Lisa's eyes following the gun. She leapt at it. Jack's gun swept right and fired. At exactly the same moment, Ned held his aim and fired. Jack fell to the ground in a slump.

Chapter Forty-Two

"All right you," Kevin said to the remaining guard. "Get on the floor."

"Somebody better check that guy and make sure he's dead." Kevin waved his head toward Jack's body.

Lisa was still on the floor in a daze. Ned stepped forward to examine Jack. The gunshot was in the center of his chest. Ned checked for a pulse. He couldn't find one.

"He's gone," said Ned.

"I take it he was one of the bad guys?" Kevin was already in the process of tying the guard's wrists.

"Indeed he was," said Ned.

"Can you keep this other guy covered until I get to him?" said Kevin. "Just in case he wakes up."

"Sure thing." Ned looked at the other man lying on the

floor. Then he looked back to the door. "Lisa, are you okay?"

Alonzo spoke up, still tied to his chair. "Yes. Are you okay Felisa?"

"I'm fine," Lisa was slowly getting up. "It's just… It was just so loud."

Ned looked back to Kevin, who was now tying the second guard's hands. Then he turned his attention to Alonzo.

"Okay," said Ned. "Here's the deal Alonzo."

"That's Colonel Madero."

Ned looked again at Alonzo. He could see the family resemblance between Alonzo and Lisa. Alonzo, however, spoke with much more of an accent than Lisa did.

Ned was now looking directly at Alonzo. "I don't recognize your army as representing a sovereign government, Mister Madero. You are an illegal combatant, so I won't refer to you as Colonel. Now here's the deal. Our mission is to take you back to the United States. You can come as a prisoner and face trial for insurrection, terrorism, and illegal warfare, or you can come with us voluntarily and testify as a witness against the CLA. In exchange, when the trial is over, you will receive a commutation of your sentence from life in prison to time served."

Alonzo stared back at Ned. "You say the American Army is already on its way?"

"That's right."

He then looked at his sister. "And you, Felisa, you're on his side?"

"I am."

Alonzo looked back at Ned. "Then where do I sign?"

Chapter Forty-Three

Both of the guards had been bound and gagged and Kevin was standing ready.

"All right," said Ned. "We need to get moving. We're all going to walk out of here and head back to the car. Kevin, cut him loose, but keep him covered." Ned motioned to Alonzo.

"Yes sir."

Ned now looked directly at Alonzo. "Kevin here is going to be right behind you during our walk. Keep in line, and don't call out to anyone, or we'll assume you've turned against us. And don't think I won't put a bullet in you if I have to. The mission is to bring you back alive, but if it looks like you're compromising it, I'll do what I need to."

"I understand."

Just as they had cut him free, they heard noise outside.

"Let's get out of here," said Ned.

The rest of the group followed him as he retreated, out the back door, over the fence, and back into the yard next door. By the time they made it to the street, Ned could see that a group of people had gathered at the front of the building. He contemplated crossing to the other side of the street before heading south again, but thought it might look too conspicuous. They walked back toward the river, past the crowd of people, when suddenly, a large explosion sounded to the east, and then another to the north, and another. The crowd went silent.

Then, Ned heard one voice in the crowd. "Los Yanquis están llegando."

That's right, thought Ned. The Yanks are coming.

Chapter Forty-Four

They continued to walk south toward the river. The sound of American artillery had almost assured that no one would be looking for them. The general disorganization of the camp had descended into complete chaos. Ned was at first concerned that they might be viewed as walking in the wrong direction, but it seemed as if most of the CLA soldiers were also heading back across the river. It was as if somebody had ordered a mass retreat, even though no one had.

They made their way quickly back to the car, and started driving away from the dam and back toward Lisa's home.

"Do you hear that?" asked Alonzo?

Ned stopped the car and listened. "Do you mean the quiet?"

"Yes."

"The artillery's stopped," said Ned. "Why?"

"That's a good question."

Ned got out of the car and took the satellite phone out of his pocket. He started calling the number for his military handler when he noticed the sound of rushing water. He looked toward the sound and saw the canal where the Acequia Madre ran. It was raging now, and it looked like it was rising.

The water was early.

Chapter Forty-Five

After speaking briefly to his handler, Ned got back into the car. By now the water was nearly past the banks of the canal.

"What's going on?" asked Lisa. "I could only hear half the conversation, but it sounds like the American Army's retreated."

"It has."

"And the water's here early?"

"It is."

"So what's going on?" asked Lisa again, with even more urgency in her voice.

"You remember from our briefing earlier, that there were two major diversion dams not too far upstream from El Paso? The Leasburg and the Mesilla."

"Yes, I remember. They weren't supposed to stop the water."

"They didn't. But what did happen, was that debris in the river caused a temporary blockage at both of those sites."

"What kind of debris?" asked Lisa.

Ned shrugged. "Trees, bushes, parts of houses. It could be anything. I imagine there are a lot of tumbleweeds. Anyway, the blockage stopped the water, at least temporarily. Then, when the dams finally did fail, the water had more hydraulic power."

"So the water moved faster," said Kevin from the back seat.

"That's right," said Ned. "The water moved faster. That's why it's already here. But the real problem, is that the same thing is happening at the site of the American Dam."

"Then the water will be moving fast again," said Lisa.

"Not just fast," said Ned. "That dam's only two miles upstream from here, so the water will be moving destructively fast. Probably fast enough to immediately overtop the international dam."

"And that's where the battle was going on," said Lisa.

"And that's why the Americans retreated."

"Then aren't we heading the wrong direction?" asked Lisa, suddenly realizing that they were driving back toward the Dam.

"There are still hundreds of people at that site," said Ned. "And with the Americans retreating, the CLA soldiers might decide to dig in. I want to give them a fighting chance before the flood hits."

"What about my people?" asked Kevin. "Do they know about this?"

"They should," replied Ned. "Captain Smith is still with them. They've taken the CLA headquarters, and that area's on higher ground. They should be fine."

"And what about us?" asked Alonzo. "How are we going to be fine if we get caught up in a flood?"

"There's high ground just south of the Dam. We should be okay, as long as we get there in time."

They arrived back at the dam. The Acequia Madre was nearly pouring out of its canal. When they moved from the lower side of the dam, to the upper side, they could see that the reservoir was already nearly full. Ned knew that even without the raging water that was coming, the dam would soon fail, just from the pressure of all the water. It was never designed to hold back such a volume of water. It had only been built to divert water into the Acequia Madre. The gates should really be opened to avoid failure, but it didn't really matter. Not with the flood coming.

Ned drove the car back below the dam and as close to the riverbed as he dared. There were still CLA soldiers crossing the riverbed in both directions. He held the radio microphone up, and looked at Lisa, Kevin, and Alonzo. "Who wants to make the announcement? I don't think they'll take me seriously with the American accent."

"Let me do it," said Alonzo. "They're my soldiers."

"Do you know what to say?"

Alonzo nodded.

Ned flipped the dashboard switch to activate the PA system and held the microphone up for Alonzo, whose hands were bound. "Go ahead."

"This is Colonol Alonzo Madero. There is an immediate threat of flood. The Gringos are in retreat because of the danger. Evacuate the area immediately. Get to higher ground or seek temporary shelter. Spread word to the command headquarters. I repeat…"

Alonzo repeated the message three times. It looked like the soldiers were taking the message seriously. Then, a group of soldiers started to head toward the car.

"All right," said Ned. "That's enough. Let's get going."

Suddenly, a growing noise arose in the distance, and the river began to swell even faster. The water was starting to spill over the top of the dam, and would soon be in the street. Ned knew the flood was coming.

Chapter Forty-Six

Ned immediately drove the car back upstream.

"We're going the wrong direction," said Lisa emphatically.

"We need to get up that hill," said Ned, and motioned with his hand to the left. There was a traffic circle ahead, but Ned crossed to the wrong side of the highway, drove past a convenience store, and turned left on an unpaved street. It went uphill steeply. Ned was glad to see that the soldiers were also evacuating the area, hastened by the rumble of the raging water. He drove the car through a maze of streets going uphill, until he found a high point with an open view.

"Why did we stop?" asked Lisa.

"I want to see it," said Ned, getting out of the car.

"See what?" asked Lisa.

"I want to see the flood. Come on." Ned moved to the

side of the road, where Lisa and Kevin joined him, and then pointed down at the river.

"You see there?" Ned pointed. "There's the dam."

"And there." Ned pointed again, this time upstream. "That's where the water will come." He was like a narrator telling a story that everyone already knew.

Then, just as Ned was lowering his hand, they could all see the water charging down the river valley. The raging water looked more like a cloud at first, with mist pouring out around the edges, but as it moved closer, there was no mistaking the motion of water."

"There it is," shouted Ned.

When the water reached the dam, it immediately poured over it, and the sound of bending steel and shattering concrete seemed like a gentle whisper compared to the awesome sound of the raging water. All of the low lying areas, including the area the CLA had been using as their command center, were now under several feet of water. They could see that many of the soldiers had been swept away.

"Will the water recede now?" asked Lisa.

"I don't expect so," said Ned. "It'll take at least an hour for most of the water to move through, and it'll probably crest in about half that time. I'm guessing, but I think it'll rise another few feet before receding."

Lisa shook her head and looked away. Ned tried to imagine her grief. He knew that she was acquainted with many of the soldiers, and that this had always been her home.

"What about the restaurant?"

Ned thought for a moment, and remembered the cook.

"The water will reach there," said Ned, gently placing a hand on Lisa's shoulder. "But Jorge should be fine. It will only rage around the river, and it shouldn't be deep enough for him to drown, even if he can't swim."

Ned looked back out over the river.

"You might need to rebuild."

"No," said Lisa. "I'm never coming back here." Then she turned to Ned and held him tightly as her tears started to flow.

By now, a small crowd of people had begun to gather. Ned, Lisa, and Kevin were all still dressed like CLA soldiers, but they also had a prisoner in the back of their car, which might draw too much attention.

"All right," said Ned. "It's time to go."

They returned to the car and Ned slowly drove the back streets to the former CLA headquarters. There, they could meet up with Captain Smith and the El Paso Valley Militia.

Chapter Forty-Seven

It was still light when they rendezvoused with Captain Smith and the El Paso Valley Militia. An army helicopter picked them up before dusk to return to El Paso. By the time that their military flight to Austin had taken off, it was after ten o'clock.

Captain Smith had filled Ned in on how the battle had gone. It had barely gotten started at the International Dam site when news of the flood caused Army Command to call back the American troops. For the El Paso Valley Militia, the engagement over the CLA headquarters had gone swiftly. The warehouse buildings were almost entirely deserted of CLA military personnel, as most of their forces were attempting to hold the border. Smith reported casualties of only seven militia men during the engagement. Once the blockage at the

American Dam site broke through, the United States Army easily took control of that location, as the CLA soldiers were in complete disarray. The International Dam site was still flooded, but the American troops had held their lines nearby where the ground was still above flood level, and were ready to take control of that area, once the waters receded. Ned heard that the dam was taken without incident before he left El Paso. After the flood, the CLA was in total disarray, with no command structure to speak of, and there really wasn't much fighting, but the United States Army was steadily occupying every region of both El Paso and Juárez, and planning on maintaining martial law until all hostilities had ceased.

Alonzo was being moved to FBI headquarters in Washington DC, where he would be held in custody until his commitment to testify against the CLA was completed. Ned, Lisa, and Kevin were all going to Austin to meet with Senator Andreaz.

The flight to Austin was quiet. Ned tried to sleep but couldn't. He found himself thinking more and more about Lisa and what she had lost.

It was after midnight when the plane landed. Senator Andreaz was waiting at the terminal, and brought them into a private room at the airport.

"Don't get too comfortable Ned," said the senator. Our flight to Washington leaves in an hour."

"Back to Washington already?" asked Ned.

"That's right," said the senator. "The president wants to pin medals on both of your chests," and he motioned toward

Ned and Kevin. "I could probably get one for you too, Miss Madero."

"I think I'll pass on the medal right now," said Lisa. "If that's okay?"

"That's just fine," said the senator. "So Ned, I have to tell you about the war."

"I heard about the battle in El Paso," said Ned. "After the flood, there wasn't much left to do."

"No Ned, not in El Paso. The rest of the fighting. The president was trying to keep it quiet up until now, but there have been multiple incursions into Northern Mexico this evening."

"Multiple incursions?"

"That's right," said the senator. "And not just into Chihuahua, but into every Northern Mexican State. He's used covert assets already in place, and delivered Special Forces units to assist them. They've captured the seats of government in nine states, and the president has issued an ultimatum to the government in Mexico City."

Ned stood wide-eyed. "What kind of ultimatum?"

"He said that if their government wanted to maintain any autonomy, they would withdraw their federal troops to Mexico City, or order them to surrender to our forces. It looks like they're mostly complying, but only time will tell how long it will take to secure all the territory we've claimed, even though the president is certain it will go quickly."

"What happens now, then?" asked Ned.

"There will eventually be some kind of peace treaty with

Mexico City. Anything less and the United Nations would be up in arms. But I'm pretty certain that the president wants to keep all of Northern Mexico as United States Territory. On top of that, the Mexican state of Yucatan has asked us to become a United States protectorate."

"Why would they do that?"

"I think they think assimilation into the United States is inevitable, and if they come in early, they might get a better deal. Regardless, any Mexican state that asks to be part of the United States will probably be accepted."

"Wow," said Ned.

"I know," said the senator.

"Anyway, there's a nice restaurant here in the airport. Let me take you all to get something to eat before our flight."

"If you don't mind Senator," said Ned. "I think I'd just like to sit for a while." The senator gave Ned a circumspect look.

"I could eat," said Kevin.

The senator shifted his gaze from Ned to Kevin. "What about you Miss Madero?" The senator said as he shifted his gaze once more.

Lisa looked at Ned, and then at the senator. "I think I'll sit here with Ned."

"All right then Mister Hirsch. Let's get going." The senator looked back again at Ned and Lisa. "I'll have the kitchen make you up some sandwiches."

"Thank you Senator," said Ned, as he sat down in a large padded armchair. Lisa sat down in the chair next to Ned as

Kevin and Senator Andreaz left the room.

This was the first time they had been alone since the plane ride back to El Paso. Ned felt like time was passing slowly. It seemed like such a long time since they had returned to El Paso, but it was, in actuality, less than twelve hours. Now, their mission was completed, and it was a different world than the one they had left.

"So Lisa, what are we going to do once all this has ended?" asked Ned, still looking forward.

"I think maybe we should run away together," said Lisa. "I hear that Puerto Rico is beautiful." She placed her hand on top of his.

"Marlene will be waiting for me. I should go back to her."

"Yes, you should."

Ned turned to look at Lisa, and then he held her hand.

***

About the Author

Chad Clabo is an independent author from Minneapolis who visits Texas whenever he can. He enjoys sopapillas and hopes to someday attend the Hatch Green Chili Festival.

Chad has dug post holes in the panhandle, battled tumbleweeds on the plains, and watched the sun set over fields of cotton. He knows the secret to making excellent King Ranch Chicken and Lefse.

When he's not writing, Chad engages in bicycle riding around the lakes of Minneapolis, weather permitting, and speculates on the potential for happiness when Lubbock Texas is in the rear view mirror.